Veronica and the Volcano

Veronica and the Volcano

Geoffrey Cook
illustrated by Gabrielle Shamsey

www.violetmoon.com

Illustrations: Gabrielle Shamsey
Design & typesetting: Shanna Compton, shannacompton.com

Published by VioletMoon
www.violetmoon.com

Paperback
ISBN-13: 978-0692894484
ISBN-10: 0692894489

Contents

Train your telescope to the edge
Of what cannot be seen but only felt
And know that everything imaginable must be.

Crater Lake

Veronica's House

Mount Mystery

Mount Mystery
and
Surroundings

Fire Bay

Dream Cove

Volcano Pearls

CHAPTER 1

In another lifetime, in a land of lava and love, there lived a young girl named Veronica. Veronica had brown hair and beautiful hazel eyes. She wore a strand of pearls every day, even to bed, because her middle name was Pearl. Veronica had a mom and dad, who loved her very much, and a little sister, Elyse, who loved to play. She was, in fact, a perfectly ordinary girl, except for one very important thing—Veronica lived on a volcano.

"Lava bomb!" Veronica called brightly from the passenger seat, as her father backed the lava car out of the garage. She heard the telltale shriek and saw the orange glow. A flaming boulder, about the size of a school desk, streaked through the summer sky.

She pressed the red button in the center of the dashboard—a button clearly marked LAVA SHIELD. The lava bomb struck with the force of a lightning bolt. Showers of incandescent stones hailed down upon them, as if from a volcanic thundercloud.

But Veronica and her dad hardly noticed. Above them, a clear lava shield rose out of the hood, extending over the car like a glass umbrella. Veronica watched the flames roar above their heads, die out, and then vanish. She pressed the red button again. This time the lava shield retracted, tucked back under the hood, and folded neatly out of sight.

"Dad, you do *really* think they'll have volcano pearls in town—don't you?" she asked.

"Absolutely—definitely, umm, maybe," he stammered, not sure at all. "But if they don't, you know you can always make her something. Mom loved your painting from last year."

Veronica rolled her eyes. "Another painting? Mom's going to be forty this year, and she needs something special—something she'll take with her everywhere she goes. Something like these." And she thumbed at the pearls around her neck.

The town of Crater Lake was a fifteen-minute drive from Veronica's house, and she knew the way by heart: Turn right at the end of the long driveway, then go another mile or two down the volcano, following the road along the riverbed for five more miles. The river spilled into Crater Lake, and the town by the same name hugged the lake's northern shore.

Both the town and the lake sat in the crater of a supervolcano. Supervolcanoes are particularly large volcanoes, of the world-ending sort, that can blanket the earth with ash and blot out the sun. Scientists say this supervolcano last erupted five million years ago, before there were any humans around to

see it. Now, these same scientists say it is extinct—completely inactive—and of no threat to anyone.

But the volcano Veronica lived on was far from extinct. It was the closest *active* volcano to the town of Crater Lake, and everyone in town heard it rumble nearly every day.

As active as the volcano was, it had no official name. The townspeople referred to it as Mount Kaboom or even just Kaboom. But Veronica's family never did. They referred to it as that Old Girl, the Red Lady, or simply She. (Veronica always thought Veronica's Volcano had a certain ring to it. But her sister, her parents, her friends, and most everyone else disagreed.)

Veronica's volcano was smaller, not at all of the world-ending sort, but worrying enough to the townspeople of Crater Lake. *Their* world, at least, could easily meet a fiery end from the right-sized eruption. Luckily, that eruption hadn't happened—at least not yet. For as long as anyone could remember, Veronica's volcano never did anything more than put on a show. Sure, it smoked every now and then, and erupted a bit of lava here and there, but that was about it.

Still, it was a volcano. The townspeople never quite understood *why* Veronica and her family chose to make their home in such an unforgiving place. But *how* they did so was no mystery.

Veronica's family had no special powers. Yes, they had guts and brains—and some special lava gadgets—but above all, they had respect for the volcano they called home. They knew when to stay, and they knew when to run. But today Veronica and her father were simply driving to town to pick up a birthday present.

The lava car rolled to a stop in front of the town's only jewelry store. Veronica hopped out and walked briskly to the entrance. She noticed the sideways sign on the door and cocked her head to read the odd words: NOT CLOSED.

She opened the door gently and saw an old man behind a counter full of glittering gems. Crooked crayon portraits decorated every wall of the store. Some hung right-side up, some upside down, and some backwards. On another wall hung a sideways mirror. Veronica smiled at her reflection and straightened her pearls.

"Excuse me, sir?" she asked politely. "Do you—err—have any volcano pearls here?"

The old jeweler said nothing. He wore dark sunglasses in the dimly lit room. He looked to be at least seventy-five years old, with hair as white as snow and teeth as yellow as the sun. A tall, stiff collar rose from his frumpy jacket. The man grasped his chin and scrunched his forehead, as if thinking of something very far away.

Veronica noticed her father quietly enter the room. She repeated her question in a louder voice. "Excuse me, sir, do you have any volcano pearls here?"

"I'm blind, girl, not deaf," he said, his voice as old and gravelly as his face. "I think we sold the last one yesterday, or maybe an hour ago, or maybe the year after the week before that. But . . . it's possible, yes, that just maybe—" The jeweler stopped. "I might have a whole drawer full . . ."

He crossed the room slowly, tapping his cane with every step. He stopped at a large chest of drawers and slid the top one open. Veronica gasped. A pale white light reflected off his dark glasses. For a moment, he looked younger, familiar, alive.

Thud. He slammed it shut. "Nope, didn't think so," he said. "But you do know where *else* you can find volcano pearls, don't you?"

"Let's go, Veronica," her father said. "It's time to leave."

The old man ignored him. "Volcano pearls are cooled lava. They are mostly black, but sometimes—sometimes—they come in different colors. And white is the rarest of them all."

"Yes, I know that," Veronica said excitedly, clutching her pearls. "My grandmother left me these. I'm wearing them, see? White ones!"

"See?" the old man said. "Can't you see? I'm in the *dark*! There was a time that I could see, and I have seen. I've seen what those pearls can do. And if you're wearing what you say you are, you're asking the wrong person for more."

"Huh?" Veronica said. "But—this is a jewelry store. Who else would I—"

"Ask your daddy," the old man said.

"Veronica, really, it's time to go," her father said again. "He doesn't have the pearls."

With wrinkled hands, the old man raised the cane high. "LOOKEE HERE!" he said, exposing a large white pearl handle. "Look familiar?"

Veronica clasped her hands to her chest. "Is that a . . . ?"

"You betcha!" he said. "The biggest one I've ever known. A child gave this to me yesterday, I think, or maybe it was to-morrow. One thing I know: Nothing on earth is rarer or more

beautiful than a volcano pearl. If you're lucky, you'll find them on the far side of Mount Mystery, somewhere in the black sands. And if you're unlucky, well . . ."

Veronica's father's face went white. "That'll be enough, sir. Thank you very much," he said, not meaning it at all.

But the old man was not finished. He bowed his head and looked at Veronica over the rim of his dark glasses. Where his eyes should have been were two hollow holes, black empty sockets.

Her mouth fell open.

"You see how evil man can be?" the old man said darkly. "When the volcano does blow, true colors will show. Nature is nature. It's always right. But man can be evil and man can be right. And man can be blinded by a terrible night. An evil is coming . . . he's coming in white!"

Veronica stood transfixed by his blind stare. Her father rushed between them. "What's wrong with you?" he said loudly. "As old as you are—scaring children—you should be ashamed. I'm sorry about your eyes, but it's no excuse."

"I'm sorry too," the old man said, and he straightened his glasses.

"Veronica! Let's go!" her father snapped. He hurried her out of the store and into the car.

Veronica wasted no time. "Daddy, where did my pearls come from? Are they *really* from Mount Mystery?"

"Uhh, well, I, uhh . . ." he faltered. "You know they were your grandmother's, so I, uhh, think you should probably ask your mother that question."

"So it's true!" she said. "Can we go? To Mount Mystery? To the far side?"

"Veronica Pearl!" he chided, hoping her middle name, sternly uttered, might end the conversation. "You know why it's called Mount Mystery. Lava is dangerous enough, but Mount Mystery is something else entirely. Violent eruptions, poisonous geysers, pyroclastic flows, lava bombs as big as houses. It's just no place for little girls," he said, cringing as the last two words passed his lips.

"But Daddy, I'm not a *little girl* anymore," she said. "I'm ten. And I *am* old enough. Where else can I find volcano pearls for Mom? The old man . . . he's right, isn't he?"

"Him? Right?" Her father laughed. "*Please* . . . he's nothing but a spooky-talk-spewing kook." He glanced away from the road and into her pleading eyes. "Veronica, listen to me, I *know* you're not a little girl anymore. And your mother would love 'em, I'm sure. I'll tell you what . . . I'll think about it."

Veronica smiled. *One parent down, one to go,* she thought. A *maybe* from her dad was as good as a *yes.* From her mom, well, that was a different story.

The lava car raced through the volcanic countryside. Veronica settled back into her seat, quietly gazing out the window, and daydreaming about the wonders she'd find in the black sands on the far side of Mount Mystery.

Ice Tires

CHAPTER 2

By the next day, Veronica had made her plan. She would climb Mount Mystery, take her best friend, Maddy, and leave tomorrow. But first, she would need her dad to help get ready, her mom to say yes, and Maddy's parents to let her go. Fortunately, Maddy happened to be sleeping over at Veronica's house that very night. *All in a day's work*, she thought.

Veronica found her dad in the garage, lying on his back, his feet protruding from under the car. "Is it ready yet?" she asked sweetly.

"Veronica, you can't just jump in a car and drive to Mount Mystery," he said in a muffled voice. "It takes preparation. It takes time. Everything needs to be perfect. Now, can you please hand me that tube?"

She grabbed a large metal hose on the garage wall and pressed it into his blindly grasping hand. "Here you go," she said. "Whatcha doin' anyway?"

"Just filling the ice tire tank," he said. "I'm not about to get stuck on Magma Pass without ice tires—not again anyhow."

Now, ice tires are not *exactly* what they sound like. They do not help with driving on ice, nor are they made of ice, but there is no better way to drive on lava. The tires themselves are titanium metal and covered in tiny pin-sized holes. When activated, supercold liquid nitrogen sprays out of the holes, coating the tires. When the liquid nitrogen touches lava, it turns to gas, forming a cocoon that prevents the tires from melting, at least for a little while.

"Dad," Veronica said, addressing his still-sticking-out feet, "Maddy's coming over for a sleepover tonight, and—well—I was wondering . . . if it would be all right with you if she came, you know—with us—to Mount Mystery tomorrow?"

"Tomorrow!" he yelled, sliding out from under the car. "You know perfectly well your mother hasn't even said she'd let *you* go—let alone with a friend. If Maddy's parents have any sense they won't let her go, and if your mother has any sense she won't let you go. But, somehow, if it turns out that nobody has any sense, then sure—why not?—at least the car will be ready."

"Ready?" Veronica said, looking over the gleaming car. "It's unplugged!"

"No it's not, I—ugh!" he groaned, noticing the empty wall outlet. "Could you please umm—?" And he slid back under the car.

She laughed. "I guess we weren't going to get very far." She tapped the license plate, and it swung open, exposing the car's power cord. She grabbed the cord and extended it to the outlet on the wall. The underside of the car glowed red.

When a lava car charges, it first glows red, then orange, then yellow, then green, then blue, until it finally glows violet when fully charged. A full charge can take five hours but, once charged, the car can travel more than a thousand miles, in normal temperatures.

Her father returned to banging and clanging, the tube clattering against the concrete floor. She waited for a break in the noise. "Daddy? Could you tell me the story of our house again?" she asked, still speaking to his feet.

"Now?" he said. "Can't you see I'm a little busy?"

"Just the short version," she insisted.

"But . . . ," he began to protest. "Fine," he sighed. Veronica's dad liked to tell the story as much as she liked to hear it. "You were just a baby. Mom and I wanted the perfect house with the perfect view for our perfect family. We were house hunting on Crater Lake. She noticed a jet of steam erupt far in the distance and took it as a sign. We drove for miles, searching for the source. And we found it—right here—next to the most magical lava-heated pool.

"We asked a local scientist to survey the land. She discovered a vast underground magma sea, flowing right under our feet. She installed a device, called a turbine, to capture the steam coming off the vent and turn it into electricity. Without that electricity to run our lava pumps, we'd all be lava toast."

He laughed, but she did not. She had zoned him out midstory, certain she'd heard the back gate slam. "It's Maddy!" she said. "She's here!" Veronica ran out of the garage, leaving her father alone under the car.

Maddy lived in the town of Crater Lake. Whenever she visited, her father dropped her off at the end of Veronica's long driveway. Maddy knew better than to ring the doorbell. When she wanted to find her friend, there was only one place to look—the pool!

Maddy and Veronica first met at the age of three, both crying in the hallways of Crater Lake Preschool, unwilling to leave their mommies. Playdates were arranged, and the girls became fast friends. They helped each other overcome their toddler fears, and they'd been helping each other ever since.

Veronica ran from the garage into the living room, where she stepped through the sliding glass door onto a stone patio overlooking a large pool. But where was Maddy? Instead, there was Elyse—her noisy, golden-haired sister—splashing and playing in the crystal-clear waters, along with her mother.

Veronica swam in the pool nearly every day, except during eruptions. Its naturally heated waters bubbled up from deep inside the earth. Even on the coldest, snowiest winter days, the pool beckoned like a warm bath. Veronica learned long ago to always be ready for a swim. She shed her clothes down to her bathing suit and ran toward the opening in the patio wall, an opening made for just one purpose: jumping in!

"Look out below!" she called. Elyse and Mom looked up, just in time to see Veronica falling through the sky in her bathing suit and pearls. A giant splash soaked them both.

"Hey, you splashed my eyes," Elyse yelled, swimming over to do something about it.

Before she could, Mom grabbed Elyse's foot and began to tickle it. "I'm going to put you in a bottle and send you across the sea," she said, pretending to do just that.

"But then I'd cry all day," Elyse said. She twisted out of her mother's grip, shooting an imaginary burst of ice powers at Veronica. Veronica returned fire.

"Mom—I've been meaning to ask you," she said. "Did Grandma find her pearls on Mount Mystery?"

Her mother's face turned deadly serious. "What? Why? Where did you hear that?"

"At the jewelry store in town," Veronica said. "The old man, he said the pearls can only be found in one place. Did they really come from Mount Mystery?"

"Well," her mother began tentatively, "you know how much those pearls meant to your grandma. She wore them every day of her life. And she'd be wearing them still if she were still with us."

Of course, Veronica knew all that already. A painting, a self-portrait of her grandmother wearing the pearls as a young woman, hung in their living room over the couch. Grandma had passed away when Veronica was nothing more than a heartbeat inside her mother's belly. Still, Veronica knew her grandma. She knew her from the stories, the paintings, and the photos. She knew her from the pearls on her neck and the Pearl in her name.

"But Mom . . ." Veronica said, "you're not answering the—"

"And why do we have to talk about sad things?" her mother said. "Can we just play three claps?"

"Fine," Veronica said, hearing the name of her favorite game. "I'll count." She shut her eyes and spun around. "Ten-nine-eight-seven-six-five-four-three-two-one. CLAP!"

Her mom and sister each clapped one time. With her eyes closed, Veronica had just three claps to find one of them, no small task in such a large pool.

As Veronica clapped again, Maddy opened the back gate. She tiptoed into the yard, ready to swim in a purple one-piece bathing suit. She shushed Mom and Elyse with her index finger to her mouth and slipped secretly into the fairytale waters. She crept to within inches of Veronica.

"Clap!" called Veronica.

CLAP!

Maddy's hands slapped together like a pistol shot. Veronica spun around and lunged at her, dunking them both. They surfaced together, coughing up water.

"What took you so long?" Veronica laughed. "I made a list of things to do: swim in the pool, make popcorn, watch a movie. Oh, and Mom, would it be all right if Maddy and I go to Mount Mystery tomorrow with Dad? Dad said it would be okay with him if it was okay with you."

"*Oh—did—he—now?*" her mother said, glaring. She did not like always having to be the bad guy, but she liked even less the thought of her daughter dead on Mount Mystery. She prepared to deliver the terrible but fairly obvious news that Mount Mystery was out of the question, that Veronica was far

24

too young, and that she should just stop asking—at least until she was sixteen, or maybe eighteen, or better yet, twenty-one.

"Well, Veronica . . ." her mother began.

A frantic shout interrupted her. Veronica's father had just stepped outside and noticed a ring of steam circling the volcano's peak like a halo in the summer sky. Then another. And another.

Steam rings, he thought. "Get inside! Eruption!" he yelled. He hit a button on the garage wall. An alarm sounded, and vast lava shields began to emerge from the roof, extending over the sides of the house like a clear awning.

But lava shields only protected the house, not the yard. Once a week the family practiced timed eruption drills. Unlike a fire drill, they did not flee the house, they fled the yard. During an eruption, there was no safer place than their living room and no more dangerous one than their backyard.

As the volcano roared, the ground rolled and the pool water waved with the rhythms of the quaking earth. The girls darted toward the house, throwing open a side door. From the living room, they watched out the window as the volcanic beast breathed fire all over their backyard.

Veronica's dad stumbled through the same door a minute later, his pants tattered and his knees bloodied. Dazed, he heard a ringing in his ears, but he picked up the phone, just in case. "Ahh, h-h-h-hello?" he managed.

"Ahh—*hallo?*—*hallo?* It's me—John!" declared the voice. "You know—Maddy's dad! What the HECK is going on? It looks like Kaboom's about to blow. Get Maddy out of there, NOW!"

Eruption

CHAPTER 3

"Daddy, look!" Veronica said excitedly, staring out the living room window.

The blue skies and yellow sun had turned black. Birds of every color flew in one direction, away from the volcano. Fiery lava gushed out in giant arcs from the volcano's peak, as ghostly steam rings stretched for miles into the wild, ash-flaked sky.

Veronica grabbed the family iPad from an end table. Two years ago, for the third-grade science fair, she had set up sensors all around her yard to measure earthquakes. Her father monitored the sensors on an iPad app that showed something like an X-ray of the volcano, how much lava might pour out, and even the temperature of the lava and the ground. The app was also connected to sensors placed by other hobby scientists on other volcanoes, including the largest active volcano of all, Mount Mystery.

Her screen told her this lava was hot—more than 1,500 degrees—hotter than an oven. The app showed a web of different-colored lava tubes deep underground, carrying molten lava all around the volcano. The red and orange tubes carried hot lava right now, while the blue ones were cold and empty. But today Veronica did not need the screen to find the lava. Outside the window, a river of fire headed straight for the house.

Still on the phone, Veronica's dad glanced down at the iPad. "That won't be necessary, John," he said. "Maddy's safe here. The Red Lady's just putting on a show. I'll call you back in a few." And he hung up.

Red-glowing rocks hurled through the sky, pounding the lava shields and rattling the windowpanes. The shields stopped the biggest bombs, but the smaller ones danced in on the wind, pelting the house like so many fireflies, blinking on and off all around them.

The approaching lava glowed dark red, almost black, punctuated by veins of orange-yellow. Trees and bushes burst into flames as the lava tongue licked ever closer. "It's coming for us," Maddy whispered, spellbound.

"No it's not," Veronica said. "The walls are space glass; they glow red hot but are safe to touch. It's the same glass that protects astronauts on spaceships. And you see those trenches around the yard? It's a lava moat. We're safe here. You'll see."

Though she had been to the house many times, Maddy had never gotten used to the eruptions, and she had never seen one quite this bad. She fidgeted with her hair, watching the trenches fill up. A garage-sized pump at the edge of the yard roared to

life, stopping the moat from overflowing. Pulsing like a metallic heart, it channeled the lava away from the house. Wave after wave of lava slid into the moat and diverted down the slope.

Veronica, meanwhile, popped a bag of popcorn in the microwave. She crunched her snack on the living room couch, watching the air ignite with lava fire. She gazed, mesmerized, as the geysers dotting the landscape erupted all at once, dancing like a choreographed fountain. Yes, Veronica loved a lot of things about living on a volcano, but she loved the eruptions most of all.

Safe in her living room, Veronica remembered the question she had asked her mother in the pool. "Mom?" she said again. "You never said . . . would it be all right if Maddy and I went to . . . umm . . . Mount Mystery tomorrow? You know, with Dad?"

"*Pfffft*." A puff of air passed her mother's lips. Her tongue pressed against the roof of her mouth, beginning to form the word *no*, just as her eyes fell on the portrait of her own mother, Veronica's grandmother, hanging on the wall above the couch.

Veronica's mother relaxed her jaw. Her mouth fell open, but no words came out. She daydreamed back ten years ago to the last moments of her own mother's life.

"Mom?" Veronica pressed. "Well, can I?"

"Veronica . . ." her mother said at last. "There's something I've been meaning to tell you about your pearls. Yes, the pearls were your grandmother's, but what you don't know is this: She found them on Mount Mystery with her dad, your great-grandpa, when she was no older than you. She wore the pearls every day of her life, just like you do now. She made me promise to give them to you, Veronica, the granddaughter she would never know. But she insisted I not tell you about Mount Mystery until the time was right. And that time is now. Yes, Veronica, *yes*, you can go. You can go to Mount Mystery."

Veronica's mouth gaped open. She held her pearls in stunned silence, not sure whether to break down in tears or to jump up with joy.

Maddy chose the latter. "Woo-hoo!" she exclaimed. "You're going to Mount Mystery!"

"No—*we*," Veronica said. "*We* are going to Mount Mystery. You have to come too."

Maddy shook her head. "You know my father will *never* allow that."

"Yes he will!" Veronica replied dramatically. "Just tell him the truth: that you are *ready*."

Maddy's dad, John, or more precisely, Captain John, was a tall, friendly man with a booming voice. For as long as anyone could remember, his family had owned the biggest boats on Crater Lake. Five days a week, he captained the lake's only steamboat, the *Minnehaha*. No man alive knew more about the lake than he.

Technically, he was Captain John the Seventeenth, although he was known around town simply as the Captain—and always with a capital C, owing both to his stature in the community and also his height. The very first Captain John was a man of legend, with a statue in town to prove it. Every firstborn boy in the family since had shared his name, including Maddy's little brother, John the Eighteenth.

"Give me the phone. Here goes nothing," Maddy said. She dialed her dad's number, then switched to speakerphone so everyone could hear. "Hi, Daddy, umm, I just wanted to let you know that we're safe now, and I love you, and, umm . . . one more thing, and it's important. I want to go, that is, I'm ready to go . . . to Mount Mystery."

She winced as she spoke the words. "You see, I'm getting older, and some kids in school have already gone. And Veronica and her dad are going tomorrow. And I want to go too!"

Captain John bit his tongue. Yes, of course, he understood she would go there someday. But that someday was not tomorrow.

"I understand that, sweetie," he began, unaware of the speakerphone. "But I don't think it makes sense for you to go with Veronica's dad. You see, he doesn't understand the volcanoes like I do. You'd be stuck up there if his gadgets broke, or, god forbid, his app crashed." He snickered, or at least he meant to. But it came out as a big, booming laugh.

"So ask him to come," Veronica whispered to Maddy. "Tell him there's room."

"Then why don't you come too, Dad?" Maddy asked. "There's plenty of room in the car."

Veronica's dad cringed. He knew that he and the Captain were from two different schools of thought—like a war between the newfangled and the old-fashioned. He imagined the long car ride to Mount Mystery and the dozens of jokes he'd hear, all at his expense. He rooted to himself quietly—*please say no, please say no*—as if concentrated wishes ought to matter.

Maddy called into the speaker, "Dad? Are you still there?"

The Captain imagined Veronica and her father both stranded on a volcano, lost and helpless, and he knew his daughter would fare no better. *They got nothing but book smarts*, he thought, *helpless book smarts*. He remembered his first trip up Mount Mystery as a teenager, and he realized Maddy would go there soon enough, either with or without him. He'd rather be standing by her side than worrying back at home.

"Yes, I'm here," he said at last. "And, yes, you can go, and, yes, I'm coming too. I'll be there—at 9:00 a.m. *sharp*. I love you."

Popcorn flew. Whooping shrieks of total joy filled the room. Maddy high-fived Elyse. Outside, the eruption sputtered to a stop. The volcano lobbed its final gob of lava down the slope.

Veronica's father stared out the window. "You'll need your sleep tonight, girls," he said. "Tomorrow, we leave for Mount Mystery."

Packing the Car

CHAPTER 4

Veronica opened her eyes to the sight of her sweet sister sliding into bed next to her. "You look like a lion," she said, as Elyse's golden hair swept up like a wispy mane.

Elyse blinked her blue eyes at Veronica. "TV, please?" she squeaked in her five-year-old voice.

Veronica reached for the remote control and turned on Elyse's favorite show, the one starring a curious monkey. While normally she would have liked nothing more than to cuddle and watch TV in bed with her sister, today she had more important things to do.

Veronica poked Maddy, who was still snoring away on a sleeping bag next to the bed. Grumbling, Maddy pulled the fluffy bag up over her head. Veronica kept prodding her, until she finally got up. They threw on yesterday's clothes and ran downstairs to the kitchen, where they encountered Veronica's mother. Veronica carried her backpack.

"Mom? What are you doing up?" Veronica asked.

She looked at her daughter as if she wanted to cry. "Veronica, are you sure you're ready? There's plenty of mystery right here on this volcano, I promise you. You don't always have to go searching for it."

"Mom, I'll be okay," Veronica said. "But I have to go. It'd be *boring* to stay home. Now, can you think of anything I'm forgetting?" And she began to rummage through her pack.

Her father entered the room. "You need your backpack, rope, sunscreen, water bottle, flashlight, bug spray, and volcano booties," he said, without a missing a beat. "The car's mostly packed—save for yours and Maddy's backpacks and, of course, anything the Captain brings."

"Check, check, and check," Veronica said. She had all of those things and more. She also had some tape, because she always needed tape, and her notebook, because she loved to draw. "And how about gas masks?" she asked.

"We'd have bigger problems if we needed those," he said. "But we do need matches, waterproof ones. We'll have to stop along the way."

"How long is the ride?" she asked.

"Five hours, but we'll do it in four," he said. "We'll park at the trailhead, then hike through the Cloud Forest. We should make the campsite by sundown. The camping hammocks are already in the car. Then, bright and early, we'll wake up, climb Mount Mystery, find some pearls, make camp again, and be back in time for the next day's supper."

"Camping hammocks?" Veronica said. "You mean we're going to sleep in the . . . trees?"

"Oh!" her father chuckled. "Did you think getting to the far side of Mount Mystery was going to be easy?"

Veronica and Maddy exchanged worried glances. The butterflies in their tummies fluttered all at once. *Maybe Mom was right to worry*, Veronica thought.

Ding-dong. The doorbell rang. It was 8:00 a.m. The Captain was predictably early.

"Oh, hi," Veronica said pleasantly. "What's that?"

"My trusty tent," said the Captain. "I figure your dad's tent is too small for all of us. Am I right?"

"Oh . . . hello there, John," Veronica's dad said. "Thanks, but I don't think we'll be needing *your* tent today. We'll be using camping hammocks. They're light and real comfortable. You're going to love them."

"I'm—sure—I—won't," said the Captain, stone-faced. He dropped the tent bag in a heap on the floor along with a number of supplies including Maddy's backpack. "I guess you've got it all worked out then. Tell me," he said, "what's your *plan* to get us over Magma Pass?"

Magma Pass, known simply as the Pass to locals, marks the high point of the Magma Skyway and the entrance to Mystery County. Perhaps the steepest road in the world, the Pass is dotted with runaway truck ramps every mile. Brakes on this road are known to not just give out, but to catch fire, so often that buckets of water line the ramps, ready to douse a big rig's flaming wheels.

No two stories about the Pass are ever the same: eruptions one day, mudslides the next. But as dangerous as it can be, on

most days Magma Pass is just another stretch of road, as boring as any in the county.

"Enough about the Pass," Veronica's mother harrumphed, eyeing the Captain gravely. "No one is going anywhere on an empty stomach."

Elyse smelled the waffles first, from all the way upstairs. She bounded toward the kitchen with her long blonde hair swooped back in a ponytail, ready for the waffle-eating ceremony. Elyse loved waffles, and she loved maple syrup even more—but she did *not* love sticky hair.

"I can't find my step stool," Elyse complained, straining to reach the hot cocoa maker.

"Look in the bathroom," her mom said.

Elyse retrieved the stool and dragged it into the kitchen, setting it near the hot cocoa maker. She inserted a packet in the machine and put a mug marked *Elyse's Hot Cocoa Mug* in place. She watched the delicious liquid pour into it, then grabbed a carton of milk from the refrigerator and filled the mug to the brim. She finished off her perfect morning drink with a bendable straw and two big marshmallows from the pantry.

Meanwhile, the rest of Veronica's family made their own special morning drinks. Her dad made cappuccino, her mom juiced grapefruits, and Veronica squeezed oranges.

The family, joined by Captain John and Maddy, ate a big breakfast, chatting about the weather, about summer reading lists, about everything except Mount Mystery.

Like clockwork, with her last bite of waffle still in her mouth, Elyse raced through the house with her hands in front of her, like a scrubbed and ready surgeon, heading for the bathroom to wash her extra-syrupy hands.

"Dad, you did remember the iPad, didn't you?" asked Veronica, gulping down her last swallow of orange juice.

"Yep, got it," he said. "Even charged it last ni—"

"The iPad?" the Captain scoffed, grabbing another waffle from the stack. "Mount Mystery is no place for an iPad."

"But we need it to—" Veronica began.

"You don't *need* an iPad" the Captain snarled. "You need your eyes and ears. You need your good senses. These devices—they spew their hum into the silence, disturbing everything and everyone—and me most of all."

"Oh, come on, John, they're not that bad," Veronica's dad said.

"Not that bad, eh?" he said. "Well I beg to differ. They take more than they give, I tell you—distracting our quiet, magnifying our cruelty, increasing our efficiency, until the whirring grinding inhumanity consumes all, and, in the end, we become no better than it—a heartless machine."

"Wow. That's a little bleak," said Veronica's dad.

"No, I'll tell you what's bleak," the Captain continued. "Back in my day, we actually learned the volcanoes. We listened to them. *We paid attention.* That's the problem with kids these days, they—"

"But Captain," Veronica's dad said, "don't you think . . . maybe . . ."

"I'm telling you what I think," he jeered. "My daddy taught me you are what you eat—and that goes for more than just food," he said, raising a forkful of waffles high. "It goes for anything that eats up your time. And what eats up more time than these godforsaken devices? If you let a machine think for you, guess what? The machine gets smarter and you get dumber."

"Give me a break, John," Veronica's dad said. "I've been up Mount Mystery before, the same as you, and I survived it before, the same as you. The iPad doesn't think for me. It's progress—like the printing press, like electricity. It shows an X-ray of the magma chamber, how hot the ground is, whether or not the pressure is rising. Just this morning I checked, and all of Mount Mystery's sensors reported normal. Without those sensors—"

"Sensors-schmensors," the Captain interrupted. "If you had any senses you wouldn't need sensors."

"Listen!" said Veronica's dad. "You can choose to remain in the past all you like, but it comes down to this: These devices do things that we simply can't do. And you know what? That's okay. That's why we carry them. That's why *people* make them."

"Oh, is that a *fact*?" the Captain sneered. "I already know how this story ends. When you run out of battery, when you're out of range, when you short that silly thing out in a stream, you're going to be a helpless baby. And I'm going to have to save you."

"But it does more than just run out of battery, Dad," Maddy chimed in. "It's good for finding yourself on a map, or even just taking pictures."

"Pictures!" the Captain spat. "Why let a screen ruin your view? What picture captures the swaying of a tree, the chirping of a bird, the roaring of a river?"

"It takes video too, Dad," Maddy said.

The Captain inhaled, readying his next tirade, when Veronica's mom raised her hands. "That's enough!" she declared. "Can the four of you *please* continue this, *ahem*, discussion in the car? It's time to go."

Veronica's dad checked the clock on the wall. "Mom's right," he said. "Girls, take your last bites. The car's out front and ready."

Outside the house, the Captain stuffed his long legs into the passenger seat.

"Here," Veronica's dad said, handing him the iPad. "We'd better keep this up front, you know, just in case you get us lost."

Veronica's mom frowned. "Be kind!" she said. "And, *please*, be safe."

Veronica heard the catch in her mother's throat and let go of the door handle. There stood her mother, her eyes watery, smiling and waving, as if she could wave away her worries. She forced a grin across her face. "Today you walk in your grandmother's footsteps," she said.

Tears welled in Veronica's eyes. She blew two kisses—one to her mom and one to her sister—then turned back to the car.

"I love you more than love!" her mother called.

"But I love you more than that," Veronica said, completing the poem she had written her parents for Valentine's Day—a poem that had since become the family's familiar farewell.

Once again, Veronica let go of the door handle. She rushed toward her mother, and gave the biggest hug a daughter ever gave a mommy.

On the Road

CHAPTER 5

Packed and ready, the lava car rolled out of the driveway at 9:00 a.m. sharp. If all went according to plan, the four adventurers would arrive at the Cloud Forest in plenty of time to set up camp.

Ten minutes into the drive, Veronica's dad read the sign on the edge of the road: TOWN OF CRATER LAKE, 1 MILE. "Hey Captain, I need to stop. You didn't bring any matches, did you?"

"No," the Captain said, frowning. "I can start a proper fire."

Veronica's dad let the snipe pass. He braked hard and swerved into a strip mall on the outskirts of town, parking in front of Magma Mart. "I'll only be a minute," he said to the Captain. "Veronica, you come with me."

Magma Mart was sandwiched smack dab in the middle of Veronica's two favorite sources of sweets in the world: the Ice Creamery on the left and the Village Bakery on the right. All three businesses were owned by the same man. Veronica called him Coach, as did everyone in town. He coached at least a half-dozen teams, from girls' softball to high school football.

"Der's my lefty," Coach barked, as Veronica entered the store. A transplant from New Lava City, Coach spoke with urban power in hard, flat tones without any inflection, except for the volume of his voice. "Beddah be wahrkin' on your slap-hittin', hey? Dat's whawt summahs are fahr! Pushin' yahself fahrder dan you can go. Stawr playahs aren'd bahrn, dey're made."

"Yeah, yeah, Coach," Veronica said, "I'm practicing." Her father tossed an eight-pack of waterproof matches on the counter. "But not today. Guess where we're going . . . Mount Mystery."

"Dat's quite the wahk," Coach whistled, as he rang them up. "Good for you. Every kid shood see Mystahry at least once. Even if it means you ain't practicin'." As they turned to leave, he called after them, "You bring me my lefty back!"

Veronica smiled. She loved her town. The townspeople were like her uncles and aunts—one big, happy family. The car pulled out on the road, and Veronica melted into her seat, settling in for a long drive.

"You know," said the Captain, "as long as we're making quick stops, I'd like to make one too. There's a grave I'd like to visit."

"What grave?" asked Veronica.

"My family's," he said grimly. "It's on the way, about two hours from here, just before the Pass. Captain John the First is buried there, and so is every other Captain John, except for me and my boy of course—not yet anyhow."

"Geez, Dad," Maddy said, rolling her eyes, "we just left. Do you have to bum everyone out already?"

Veronica's dad glanced away from the road and into the Captain's grey eyes. He could tell he was somewhere else. "That sounds fine, John. I'd be happy to stop. I think I know the place—near Babeltown, right?"

"That's right!" said the Captain. "You know that old dustbin?"

"Know it?" he said. "I grew up there. It's where I met my wife. And it's where I'd be right now if it hadn't burned."

Veronica detected the twinge of sadness in her father's voice. "You know we can't control the volcanoes, Dad," she said.

Just then, the car rounded a bend, and the sapphire waters of Crater Lake rippled into view. The lake filled a basin thirty miles long by five miles wide, speckled with forest-covered islands and ringed by sheer-faced mountainsides. "Maddy, look!" Veronica yelled. "The *Minne*!"

The girls watched the proud steamboat, the *Minnehaha*, lumber up the southern shore, beating the water with its gigantic paddle wheel. Behind the *Minne*, the rocky cliffs of Diamond Island glinted in the morning light. A small chapel marked the island's southern shore. Great green groves of paper birch, silver fir, and white pine stretched to the water's edge.

"That's the sunrise Catch-and-Cruise," Maddy said, eyeing the fishing poles dotting the decks. "Uncle Ned must be piloting today." Every weekend morning in the summer, troves of hobby fishermen tried their luck in some of the richest salmon-stocked waters in the country.

"Captain, about the grave . . ." Veronica said. "Can I ask you something? How did Captain John the First *really* die?"

"Veronica Pearl!" said her father sharply. "That's no business of yours. That's for sure. We do *not* stick our noses in other people's family business."

"But it's not just his business," she protested. "It's history. Captain John the First has a statue in town! And we're going to his grave! Don't you want to know?"

"There, there," the Captain said, rescuing her. "Too many stories get told and retold, and everyone's truth is different, but I believe what my daddy told me—that an evil man came from far away. He built an army and a navy. He conquered everything from Crater Lake to Mount Mystery. Many called him a pirate, others a king."

Veronica laughed, watching the scene out her window. "What would a pirate want with Crater Lake? A pretty view?"

"How about diamonds?" the Captain said. "Loads of diamonds. Tell me—how do you think Diamond Island got its name?"

Veronica sniffed. "Oh, please! There are no *diamonds* on Diamond Island. It got its name because it's shaped like a diamond."

Like everyone else, Veronica had heard the legend of the island's diamond riches. She and her friends had searched the island many times, snorkeling, digging, and generally turning over every stone. But she never found a single gem.

Veronica had learned to dismiss the stories as myth—made up to inspire schoolchildren and confound hapless treasure

seekers who'd never grown up. From time to time, the *Crater Lake Gazette* would cover another poorly funded expedition to scuba dive the depths of Crater Lake, all 1,948 feet of it. They would always find the same thing—nothing at all.

By now, all respectable people knew that there were no diamonds on Diamond Island. Yet here was Captain John, pillar of the community, sounding like a schoolboy.

"Whose story is this?" he bristled. "You asked me what I believe, and I'm telling you. Five hundred years ago, Diamond Island was full of diamonds—more diamonds than you could ever imagine. I believe the pirate, this Diamond King, ripped them from the land. I believe Captain John, my great-great-great-great-great-great-great-great-great-great-great-great-great-great grandfather, died trying to stop him.

"And I believe his bones would lie there still—deep beneath the lake's blue waters—were it not for his friends. They rescued his body, and they buried him, properly, at a gravesite that even the Diamond King himself could not find."

"Come on!" said Veronica. "That's not true. We learned about it in school. I even visited the statue on a field trip. I know what it says."

Veronica recalled the large bronze statue of Captain John, wielding a sword against time and the elements. It stood on a hill on the lake's southern shore, with an inscription that read: CAPTAIN JOHN—FOR BRAVERY AGAINST SAVAGERY.

"He died fighting Indians," Veronica said. "Everyone knows that."

"Everyone is wrong," the Captain said, as if he believed his own far-fetched tale. "Sometimes you win by losing. Nearly undone by someone so simple, the pirate, this Diamond King, went berserk, murdering people by the thousands. It didn't take long for the story of Captain John and his small band of believers to spread. And when it did, his bones became a symbol and his name a battle cry.

"The pirate did all he could to smash the symbol, to find the grave of Captain John and erase his memory from the earth forever. But he never did. In the first light of dawn, some forty years later, Captain John's own grandson stood at the front of a one-hundred-boat armada, determined to stop the evil pirate once and for all.

"But there was no fight. The pirate vanished into the vast and hazy stillness of dawn, as quickly as he had come, like a ghost in the mist. And once gone, it was as if he had never existed at all. Not a single painting or likeness of him has ever been recovered. And what's worse: not a single diamond has ever been found. The diamonds, like the pirate, became just another myth—a tall tale told by old men to disbelieving schoolchildren."

"Well, count me as one of those," said Veronica, laughing, although she wasn't so sure. She remembered the blind old man's warning: *An evil is coming . . . he's coming in white.* If the Captain was right, an evil had already come once to her town. *Maybe it could come again,* she thought. "Daddy, what do you believe?" she asked.

"I believe the Captain, sweetie, minds his own family's business better than you," he said, without answering her at all. "Now, would you please get some sleep? We have a hundred miles until the next stop, and a long hike ahead of us."

The girls played on the iPad instead. The two men sat in silence, watching the hills roll by and the blue skies fade to grey. The car climbed a high ridge, overlooking a bleak valley. Just ahead of them lay the graves of Babeltown and the gateway of Magma Pass.

Babeltown

CHAPTER 6

Veronica looked out the window, daydreaming with her elbow on the door and her head in her hand. Maddy fiddled with the iPad, unaware of the towering city rolling into view just ahead of her.

Veronica's eyes rose above the clouds. "Daddy, does it really touch the sky?" she asked. The clouds hiding the city's peak parted—answering her—with an emphatic *yes*.

Babeltown, a once-proud city of thousands, looked more like a brightly colored painting in which all the colors had run together. Some of the houses were narrow, others wide, together covering the mountain in a twisted free-form pile stretching to the heavens. Thousands of windows looked out in every direction like so many eyes peering down upon the valley below.

"I thought for sure this place would have burned," Veronica's dad marveled. He parked the car next to a walking path and

switched off the ignition. "Okay," he said, "everyone . . . out! The old house, if it's still there, should be right up that hill. And if there's time," he added, with a wink to the Captain, "maybe we'll even stop by that grave."

Maddy stepped out of the car first, directly into six inches of ash. "Ugh! This stuff is everywhere," she whined. She removed her shoes and banged them together, shaking out the ash. She slipped them back on, bending down to retie the laces. As she did, she noticed a white field pansy flecked with grey. She picked the flower, blew off the ash, and handed it to Veronica.

"Dad?" Veronica asked, as she sniffed the pansy. "Why did you leave? This place looks nice."

"This place *was* nice, Veronica. The nicest. But things got bad—" He froze, his boot jerking to a stop just above the most perfect white blossom. "And you see that!" he said. "Another flower! More signs of life! Someday, even this town will recover."

Maddy watched a scavenging bird exit the broken windowpane of another empty house. "Well, it looks like a ghost town to me," she said, without noticing that Veronica's dad had stopped. She bumped into him, and he stumbled forward, trampling the wildflower under his boot.

"So much for your recovery," the Captain said.

Up close, the brightly colored, crooked cottages revealed the tragedy of the town's final moments. Every third house or so was nothing more than a colorful shell, hollowed out by fire. The exterior walls had withstood the flames, but the inside was burnt to a crisp.

Veronica's dad knocked against one of the walls. "Back then, we used special paint," he said. "Totally fireproof. It worked great, unless the fire started on the inside . . .."

Along the way, Maddy found a deep patch of pristine grey ash and could not help herself. "Ash angel!" she said. She fell backward, spreading her arms and legs, creating the contour of a perfect grey angel.

The Captain's jaw dropped. Before he could say a word, both Veronica and her dad fell backward too.

"Come on, Dad!" Maddy called, still fanning her arms and legs. "You'd make the biggest one of all!" But the Captain just shook his head.

Veronica's dad stood, admiring his angel. He brushed the ash from his pants and shirt. He noticed the Captain fuming, and he turned to the girls. "The house is just up there. The next green one around the bend."

At that, Veronica and Maddy peeled themselves out of the ash—so as not to disturb their angels—then raced down the path, stopping at the proud, wooden door of a dusty green house.

"Should we knock?" Maddy said, as the men approached. Veronica didn't think so. She pushed the door open and stepped through the doorway, as if stepping back in time. Inside, a newspaper dated ten years ago lay open on the counter. A dinner, served but not eaten, disintegrated in plates on the carefully set table. At the foot of the table, a high chair, covered in dried baby food, lay toppled on its side.

Veronica's dad led them down the hall to the open door of his own bedroom. Photos on the wall told the story of a young couple who fell in love, got married, and had a baby girl. He dusted off his wife's jewelry box and opened it, finding it chock-full of gleaming trinkets and heirlooms.

"Your mom's going to *flip* when she sees this," he told Veronica. "We left in such a hurry. She only took one piece of jewelry—your pearls. Your grandma always made such a to-do about that silly necklace—your mom couldn't leave it behind."

"But why?" Veronica asked. "Why did Grandma care so much?"

"Well, your grandmother always was kind of a strange bird," he said. "She believed the pearls had special powers—that they helped her in ways no one could understand."

"What kind of powers?" Veronica asked.

"Your guess is as good as mine," he said, "maybe even better. But she's hardly the first person to think so. Doctors have long known that the black ones can stop certain poisons. Although, if you ask me, I don't think the white ones do anything at all. You've been wearing yours nearly your whole life. You'd think if they had any special powers you'd know it by now, wouldn't you?"

Veronica nodded, although she was not sure at all that she would. "But why leave this stuff here?" she asked. "Why didn't you come back?"

"It was too painful," he said, and she could tell by his voice it was painful still. They walked toward the closed door at the end of the hallway. Veronica turned the doorknob.

The room had a picture window, violet walls, and the word VERONICA spelled out in large capital letters. A knitted blanket lay draped over the railing of a chestnut brown crib. A photograph of a lava river spilling into the ocean decorated one wall—and a handwritten poem decorated another. They walked to the large window, its panes long ago broken, and looked out across the blighted landscape of parched and broken trees.

Veronica noticed her father's chin wobble. "Daddy, what happened?" she asked.

He looked out the window and remembered:

Veronica, this was our home. You were my baby, and this was your room. Miles of raspberry fields fanned out in every direction. Wildflowers grew in waves of red, purple, and yellow, as far as the eye could see. Starlings chirped at your window at daybreak, just to hear you babble and coo. Your mother and I grew up here, fell in love here, and planned to raise you here.

But the volcanoes had other plans. The earth quaked, fire lit the sky, and the ash fell like snow. We would go to bed, wake up, but morning never came, just more blackness and ash—a never-ending night.

Babeltown was supposed to be safe. The nearest active volcano was more than seventy miles away, or so we thought. No one, not even the old men, could remember that volcano across the valley emitting even a waft of smoke—until it erupted.

We watched our friends and neighbors pack up and leave. The ones who stayed turned desperate, fighting over scraps of food and looting empty houses, which weren't always empty.

Hunger struck hard, and even the good people hardened. Break-ins became common. You protected your family first and your friends if you could, but you took from everyone else. Yes, everyone knew stealing was wrong, but so is watching your baby starve.

If only the day would break, we told ourselves, we could rebuild this town and return to our simple lives. But the long night never ended.

The weather changed. The ash electrified the air, and the lightning came, smashing roofs and setting house after house ablaze. We had to go. But when we tried to leave, the car wouldn't start. We masked your face and ran. We left everything behind, except for your pearls. I never looked back—until today.

Veronica's head spun. She could not imagine a town gone mad, turning on each other, fighting over food. "But I don't understand," she said. "Why do we live on a volcano then—after all that?"

"It's the life we were made for, Veronica," he said, still staring out the window. "We could have let it wreck us, but we didn't. Babeltown taught us the best we can do is all we can do. We live on a volcano because we love it, because it's beautiful, and because we can.

"Ten years ago, we had no lava shields, no space glass, no lava cars, no sensors. Now we do. We lost our home, but we made a new one. Where else would we go? There is no safe place—nowhere is beyond nature's grasp. We are a part of nature, and the volcanoes are a part of us. Your mother and I—we chose to live our lives—and not to live in fear."

Captain John listened outside the door, then cleared his throat as if to say, *It's time to go.*

Veronica squeezed her father's hand. One last time, they stood together at the old window looking out, imagining what might have been.

The *thud-thud-thud* of Maddy's feet on the stairs snapped them back to the present. Upstairs, Maddy had just finished exploring the bird's-eye view from the rooftop deck. She detected not a single graveyard. She bounded into Veronica's old room. "Hey, where is this grave, anyways?" she asked. "Are you *sure* it's around here?"

Veronica's dad dabbed his eyes. "Oh, uh, I don't know," he mumbled.

"What do you mean you don't know?" Maddy said. "I thought you grew up here."

"I did grow up here," he said. "And, yeah, I heard the rumors of that old grave. But that's all they were—rumors."

"The grave is real enough," said the Captain. "Now come with me."

The four of them walked back through the green door and onto the streets of Babeltown . . . but not before Veronica grabbed the poem off the wall and the blanket from the crib.

The Gravesite
CHAPTER 7

"It's not much further," called the Captain to the girls, who dawdled behind him chatting and kicking stones. They passed one abandoned shell of a house after another, until finally the Captain stopped. "It's just through that door," he said, his voice soft and solemn.

"But this isn't a grave?" Veronica said.

The house looked much like every other house, but one thing stood out—the door. Or more precisely, the double doors. Two bronze doors—worn, weathered, and covered in a moss of rust—seemed to tell a story. But what story? Veronica was not so sure. Carvings of two bronze angels faced each other, floating over a bubbling lake. A diamond-shaped knob jutted out of each door, daring entry.

"Is this a tomb?" Veronica's father asked, but the Captain said nothing. He dug in his pocket for a large skeleton key and placed it in the keyhole. The lock screeched like fingernails on a chalkboard. Both girls pushed, but the door would not budge. The two men pressed their shoulders to it, opening the door just enough for the group to slip through, one at a time.

Veronica looked around the dark chamber, its windows sealed from the inside. The sun shone brightly through the cracked-open doors, revealing an empty room with a staircase leading deep down into the darkness. A rat's tail slipped out of the sun and into the shadows.

Veronica stashed her poem and blanket on the floor. "We don't have to go down, umm, *there*, do we?" she asked. "I mean, I didn't even bring my flashlight."

The Captain unzipped his backpack and handed each girl a headlamp. "Here, put these on," he said. "You'll need them."

From the topmost stair, Veronica felt a cool, moist breeze upon her face. The stairway had no railings and no walls, and, it seemed, no bottom. She pointed her headlamp at the next stair, knowing her first wrong step would be her last. The four descended more than one thousand steps into the abyss, the air growing damper with each one.

At the bottom, Veronica looked up. She ran her hands along the walls, exploring the narrow passage. "Is this stone?" she asked.

"Yes, and watch your head," said the Captain, crouching. "This is a cave. You must mind two things: water and falling rock."

Veronica squeezed her father's hand, not quite sure how to mind either. She kept her lamp focused on the ground in front of her, afraid to discover what strange life-forms might be oozing and slithering on the ceiling, just inches from her head.

The Captain straightened his hunched back. "There!" he said. "You should be able to stand now." He beamed his headlamp into the darkness, illuminating still more darkness.

Veronica looked up. "How high is this?"

"You'll see," the Captain said. "Soon enough."

But Veronica could not see anything. She could only hear and feel. A river of water rumbled through the cave like a locomotive, misting and soaking the dark air. She brushed at imagined creepy crawlers on her skin. *It's only my imagination*, she told herself. *It's only my imagination.*

Ten minutes deeper into the darkness, they turned a corner and found the light. A shaft of sunlight flooded in from an opening in the distance, revealing a cathedral of stone. In front of them, giant stalagmite towers jutted out from the ground, while massive stalactite spikes dripped from the ceiling. Along the side, an impossibly fast river tore through the limestone rock.

Veronica fixed her gaze straight up at the thousands of knife-sharp spikes dangling overhead. "Look out!" she cried.

Captain John laughed. "What—the stalactites?" he said. "They've been here a thousand years, and they'll be here a thousand more."

Veronica took advantage of the dim light to look around. "Well, at least there's no bugs," she said. In fact, there was no life at all—just rock, dirt, and water. But as they approached the light, patches of fern and moss sprouted out of the stone, gradually thickening into a great green welcome mat, rolling out of the light and into the dark.

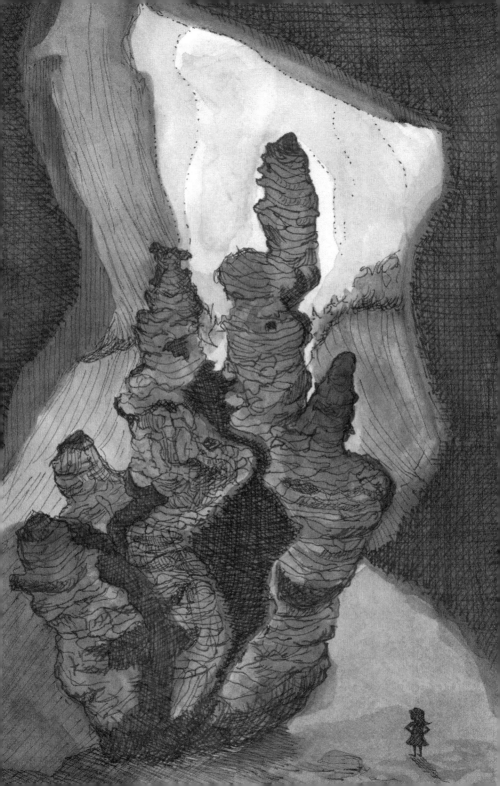

The Captain stepped first into the shimmering jungle, squinting in the glare of the noontime sun. "This is a doline," he said. "It's like a skylight in a cave. A long time ago, the cave ceiling above us weakened and collapsed, dropping millions of tons of rock right here, and forming that hill in the middle. The collapse let in the sun," he explained. "We're in an underground jungle, one thousand feet beneath the surface. The cave continues just on the other side."

Veronica marveled at the strangeness of this rock world. Somehow many of the plants and trees grew out of solid stone stems and trunks. Even the rocks grew toward the sun in bizarre forms, as stalagmites bigger than skyscrapers emerged alongside the tallest, skinniest trees.

Just ahead of her, a hairy, fantastically long caterpillar undulated across the jungle floor on hundreds of tiny legs. Veronica looked up at the sun, flabbergasted at the life-breathing magic of the ancient star.

The four adventurers scrambled up the central hill. Sixteen different headstones, each of equal size, marked the lives of sixteen different Captain Johns. At the top of the hill rested the bones of Captain John the First. The Captain dropped to one knee and read the headstone aloud:

To think the game is lost
Because you cannot win,
Forgets the grave
And commits the gravest sin.

A rustle of leaves disturbed the sacred moment. The rustling became a shaking, spreading from tree to tree, until every tree in the doline shook as one. "It's just the wind," Maddy said, hoping.

Then the shaking became a flapping. "RUN!" the Captain called. "Back to the cave! NOW!"

The flap, flap, flapping grew louder by the second. Great, inky shadows—like pterodactyl wings—danced and grew bigger on the ground beneath them.

The air beating on their necks sent shivers up their spines. They raced toward the cave, the imagined talons scraping their necks, urging them faster and faster, and still they raced, the cave just a step away, and they dove, landing spread-eagle on the cave floor.

The flapping went silent. "What was that!?!" Maddy panted. "What was that!?!"

The Captain was speechless.

From her belly, Veronica peered out of the shadows into the treetops. In the leaves of the largest tree, she thought she saw a sparkly, emerald green . . . something moving ever so slightly.

"Captain," Veronica said, "I need your binoculars. I . . . think . . . I . . . see . . ."

"Can we go?" Maddy said, eyeing the stalactite spikes above their heads. "I've just about had it with this place."

The Captain handed Veronica the binoculars. She focused on the treetop. "I think I see . . ." she whispered.

A rustle in the stunted brush made her look away. A white, fluffy blur emerged, running straight for them.

"It's a bunny!" Maddy yelled.

Veronica grasped at it but missed. The bunny's soft fur brushed past the bare skin of her legs. It hopped forward a few feet, then stopped, taking turns staring adoringly at Veronica then Maddy.

"I'll catch it," Maddy said. And the two girls took off running, with their fathers following close behind.

Each time the bunny did the same trick, hopping just out of reach, daring the girls to follow it deeper and deeper into the cave. A few hundred feet from the doline entrance, the bunny stopped. It stared once more. Veronica stooped down, and this time managed to grab it. She lifted the bunny gently with both hands.

The roar of rending rock reverberated off the chamber walls. Millions of tons of stalactites plunged thunderously to the cave floor, crashing to the ground precisely where they had stood just moments before.

"The bunny saved us!" Veronica said. "Can we keep her?"

Veronica's father stood still as stone. If not for the bunny, they all would have been crushed—entombed in a rocky grave forever, as if they had never existed at all. His first thought was of his wife—spending her remaining days searching for a family she would never find.

"Please, Dad, can we keep her?" Veronica repeated.

"Umm, err, I—" he stammered, "that is, I'm not sure your mother wants us to, umm, bring home a pet," he resisted meekly. But he knew he could not let that bunny go—not with Magma Pass and Mount Mystery still to come. "Okay, okay," he said. "We'll bring her . . . if she'll come."

And come she did. The bunny hopped between Maddy's and Veronica's feet through the darkness of the cave and back up the unrailed staircase to the strange house where it all started.

"I'm never going to another grave with you people again," Veronica's dad declared. He stepped through the bronze doors onto the streets of Babeltown. "Tell me Captain, do you have any other *quick* stops you'd like to make along the way?"

The Captain said nothing. They hiked in silence to the car. Veronica whispered into Maddy's ear: "I can't be sure . . . but I think I saw something in the tree . . . a butterfly queen!"

Maddy imagined a human-sized butterfly living in a secluded rock world and wondered: *Could the flapping have been a flutter?*

The four of them piled back into the lava car. "Dad, can we stop here again on the way back?" Veronica asked.

"No," he said sharply. "Now buckle your seat belts. Next stop—Magma Pass."

Veronica, Maddy, and the bunny settled into the backseat. Veronica lifted the bunny to her face, searching its eyes for the answer to an unknown question.

"That's it!" she said. "We'll call her . . . Lucky Bunny!"

Perfectly content, Lucky Bunny blinked, then licked Veronica's nose.

Magma Pass

CHAPTER 8

"Girls, look!" the captain said, tapping the passenger-side window. Veronica glanced up from her iPad just long enough to read the sign.

MAGMA SKYWAY

OPEN JUNE TO SEPTEMBER

ENTER AT YOUR OWN RISK!

"Why's it only open in the summer?" Maddy asked.

"Too much snow," the Captain said. "Over twenty feet a year! No snowplow dares work this high. The snow comes in October and stays until May—unless the lava melts it sooner, of course."

"There won't be any lava today," Veronica's dad said. "We'll be over the Pass in no time. For now, enjoy the view. Just let me know if you see anything weird."

"What do you mean *weird*?" Veronica asked.

He didn't answer. He swiped the car's screen, displaying a colorful map of the surrounding ground. Green patches denoted normal temperatures, yellow above 120 degrees, orange above 500 degrees, and red above 1000 degrees.

"I've never seen the screen so yellow," Veronica said. The Captain glanced at the newfangled screen exactly once, focusing his attention wholly on the road.

But Veronica's dad was fixated on the screen. He fiddled with the radio and pushed the pedal to the floor.

A high, shaky voice rasped long-haired poetry through the speakers—something about castles burning.

"Turn it down," Veronica grumbled. "No oldies, please!"

Her father ignored her, zigzagging up one of the narrowest roads on Earth. A one-lane dirt road, the Magma Skyway lacked any lane markings or guardrails. It climbed relentlessly up a volcanic plateau, one dangerous switchback after another.

Maddy noticed the out-of-place floral arrangements, "Who put the flowers on the bends?" she asked. "And what do the crosses mean?"

"Oh, they're nothing," Veronica's dad said. "You can play on the iPad now if you like."

Veronica braced herself as the car skidded into another hairpin turn—the iPad the furthest thing from her mind. She could feel the centrifugal force pushing her into the door, as if she were riding on a roller coaster. The steel of the door handle pressed into her belly. Her stomach tightened, and she began

to sweat. She closed her eyes, as if trying to escape, but the scratchy whine of the radio was too much.

"Dad! Enough!" she exploded. "You're driving TOO FAST. What if another car is coming? And the flowers! They mark death at every turn—and YOU KNOW IT!"

Her father turned off the radio. "Veronica, please!" he said. "If there were another way to Mount Mystery, I'd take it, but there isn't. I want to get off this road as much as you. But you have to calm down. This car never let us down before, and it's not going to today." His voice softened. "Besides, I'd see other cars in plenty of time on this screen. Everything will be fine. I promise."

Veronica's stomach was doing backflips. The curvy road was too much. She cracked her window, then opened it all the way. Maddy squeezed her hand. Veronica closed her eyes and stroked Lucky's soft fur. She breathed in the fresh air, exhaled all her worries, and blinked open her eyes.

The trees beyond the window grew smaller as the car climbed higher. They looked more like tree flags than trees, with all the branches sticking out of one side, as if blowing in a stiff wind. *If something as delicate as a tree could live up here,* Veronica thought, *it can't be too dangerous.*

The trees disappeared as they climbed still higher. "The top is just ahead," the Captain said. "This is the treeline, the boundary above which no tree can grow. It's too cold, too windy, and too high."

Veronica felt instantly worse. Then she saw the sign, its rusted edges waving back and forth in the howling wind:

"The top!" she yelled. "We made it!"

But rather than descend, the road leveled off onto a vast plain. Dozens of spectacular rock towers rose out of the ground, some more than a thousand feet high. Purple lilac carpeted the tundra, amidst yellow grasses and brown stones. Furry bison, white elk, and mountain goats dotted the landscape, grazing under billowy clouds and deep blue skies.

"We didn't make anything yet," the Captain said, eyeing the rock towers. "We're still above treeline—totally exposed."

Exposed to what? Veronica thought to ask. But she didn't really want to know. She just wanted to feel better. Her motion sickness finally subsided as the road straightened. She sniffed the sweet fragrance of wild lilac and admired the rock pillars that pointed to heaven beneath a golden sun. "How did these towers get here, anyway?" she asked.

"They're called lava necks," the Captain said, "and they're formed by volcanoes. Sometimes the magma in the center of a volcano's pipe hardens into rock. Rain and snow erode the soft outer rock, leaving only the solid magma core—the lava neck."

"Can they erupt?"

"Can and do," the Captain said. "The magma hardens, but if there's enough pressure underground, the whole tower can blow. Lava necks are unstable and totally unpredictable."

Now, both girls studied the towers, searching for anything *weird*.

Maddy craned her neck straight up. "A goat!" she said. Just a hundred feet away, a white mountain goat picked its way precariously to the pointed tip of the tallest pillar, where it stopped, still as stone, like a guard in its watchtower.

"Mountain goats are some of the most sure-footed animals in the world," the Captain narrated. "They climb the steepest cliffs and make leaps no human would ever—"

"NOOO!!!" Maddy gasped. The mountain goat tumbled from its perch, plummeted off a ledge, and bounced off the tundra floor—broken—amidst the wildflowers.

The lava car spoke. A female, robotic voice droned: *"Eruption—danger—eruption—danger."*

A buzzer sounded. The car's windows closed, and its lava shields deployed. The girls' attention focused on the screen in the center of the dashboard. The tower of the fallen goat lit up in orange.

"Daddy, I'm scared!" Veronica said. For the first time in her life, she watched the car's speedometer break ninety miles per hour. Suddenly, the lava neck's topmost spire crumbled and crashed.

The boom sent the bison scurrying. A one-ton buffalo stampeded straight for them. Veronica buried her face in her hands. The lava car swerved, missing the beast so narrowly that its saliva misted the side window.

The earth heaved and rolled, exploding with a thunderous roar. A thick grey pyroclastic cloud of hot pulverized rock erupted high into the summer sky. Veronica covered her ears, overwhelmed by the enormity of the sound.

Two hundred miles away, Veronica's mother was playing dollhouse in the playroom with Elyse. She heard the distant rumble. On this cloudless day, she knew what it meant. *Please,* she thought, *please be off the Pass.* She remembered Veronica's hug and prayed it would not be the last.

The Captain turned to the backseat. "Girls," he mouthed shell-shocked, as if in slow motion. "Are you okay?" He watched his daughter's faraway eyes focus on the fearsome cloud billowing just outside her window.

The car noticed their predicament: "*External air toxic. Air filters and oxygen tank activated.*"

The screen flashed the levels of the poisonous gases spewing into the atmosphere. A single breath would sear their lungs and bring instant death. Veronica's dad buried the accelerator to the floor. The glowing cloud loomed large in the rearview mirror. "It's going to be okay," he said. "We can outrace it."

"But Daddy," Veronica said, looking out the back window, "the cloud—it's getting closer . . ."

Wolf Creek
CHAPTER 9

The sky turned black as the pyroclastic cloud chased them across the Pass. A sea of fire glowed incandescent behind the angry cloud. Elbows of lightning crisscrossed its murderous face. "Faster, faster!" Veronica screamed. The speedometer crossed one hundred miles per hour. "It's getting closer," she groaned.

Veronica's dad checked the screen. The cloud was 750 degrees and moving 150 feet per second. He opened a red safety cover on the dashboard, exposing a silver toggle labeled BOOSTERS. He flipped the switch. The car rocketed across the tundra at 180 miles per hour. With one eye on the rearview mirror, he watched as the ash cloud disappeared into the distance.

"Well, that was a little close," he admitted. "But we're safe now—we'll be out of here in no time." The car continued rocketing down the road, putting ever more distance between

themselves and the cloud. "There! Look there!" he shouted. "Wolf Creek! The way out!"

Wolf Creek marked the end of the plateau and the eastern boundary of the Magma Skyway. The road ran parallel to the creek, meandering down the plateau to a tunnel at the bottom. At the tunnel, the road crossed under the creek, turning into a four-lane highway on the other side. Veronica's father knew if they could just make it to that tunnel, they'd be safe.

Out of nowhere a torrent of lava bombs slammed into the windshield. The car noticed. "*Visibility 0%. Please mind the screen.*"

Now all eyes, even the Captain's, focused on the screen. The lava car appeared as a blinking white dot, winding its way down a brown road at high speed—its passengers reduced to characters in an all-too-real video game. A curvy blue line, labeled WOLF CREEK wound next to the road.

"Lava bomb!" Maddy called, hearing the telltale shriek. The flaming rock crashed just beyond the car, setting the surrounding trees ablaze. In the flittering light, Wolf Creek's waters raged with splintered trees and ash.

"Do you hear that?" Veronica said. A small sound, at first barely audible, grew to a grinding roar. Veronica covered her ears. The Captain peered expressionless into the electrified blackness, searching for the source of the sound.

"MUDSLIDE!" he yelled. "STOP THE CAR!"

The car screeched to a halt on the overflowing banks of Wolf Creek. Millions of tons of mud and rock slid down from the plateau. Boulders, some the size of houses, blocked the road. The ash cloud grew ever closer.

"We're trapped," Veronica said. An alarm buzzed. Four sets of eyes focused on the blinking white dot at the center of the screen. A red dot flashed onto the screen's edge, then another and another. The dots became a line, snaking ever closer. It could mean only one thing—a river of lava heading straight for them.

A bolt of lightning lit up a nearby sign. Veronica read it aloud: "*Runaway Truck Ramp.* Go up it!" she called to her dad. "The lava can't get us up there."

"But the ash cloud will," he said.

Still, he pointed the car up the gravel ramp. The ramp looked exactly as Veronica imagined it would. Buckets of water lined its edge, ready to douse a big rig's fiery wheels. Only today, the water in the buckets was boiling. Veronica read the outdoor temperature off the dashboard. "It's 225 degrees!"

From atop the ramp, the Captain watched the lava river rage toward them. On the screen, the thick red line and the orange cloud converged on their blinking white dot. "We're trapped," he said. "If the lava doesn't kill us, the ash cloud will."

"Nothing's going to kill us," Veronica's dad said. "I have a plan."

Thirty seconds ticked by, then sixty. His plan, it seemed, was to do nothing. The deafening ash cloud splintered dozens of trees every second, but the lava reached them first. An inferno of flame rushed past the bottom of the runaway ramp, heading straight for the mudslide roadblock.

The Captain turned to the backseat. He took his daughter's hand. "I love you," he told her. "I love you."

"Let's not say our goodbyes just yet," Veronica's dad said. "Watch."

The lava river collided with the mudslide roadblock, sweeping away trees and ash. But the largest boulders did not budge. Millions of tons of rock continued to block the road. The lava pooled in front of the boulder dam, deepening by the second.

"Well . . . I guess we'll need to help it along," Veronica's dad said. "I thought the lava would clear the road, but no matter . . ." He reversed the car off the ramp into eighteen-inch deep lava.

"*Lava Drive Mode activated. Two minutes until car melt,*" the car droned.

The lava car's tires steamed like ice on a hot pan. The ice tires slowed the melting, if only for a moment. Veronica's dad rammed the roadblock again, but the boulders held firm, and the lava deepened.

"Daddy!" cried Veronica. "It's up to my window!"

On the car's screen, Veronica's father tapped an icon of a boat.

"*Lava Boat Mode activated. One minute until car melt,*" the car alerted.

The ice tires folded up as space-glass bars extended all around the vehicle. An air thruster tank popped up in back, providing steering. The car lifted off the ground, floating in four-foot deep lava.

"We're going to die, aren't we?" Maddy said.

"No," Veronica's dad said, shaking his head. "Not in this car." He fired the thruster and aimed for the roadblock a second time. "Here goes nothing."

He flipped the booster switch once more, and again they collided with the roadblock, this time at fifty miles per hour. The front and rear airbags deployed in their faces. Veronica's nose bled on impact. Still, the boulders held firm.

"*Ten seconds until car melt,*" the car warned. "*Climate control compromised.*"

"Daddy! It's hot!" Veronica shrieked, the sweat pouring down her face. "The floor—it's glowing!"

"Then sit cross-legged!" yelled her father. The interior temperature of the car shot from 72 degrees to 105 degrees in a few seconds. Half of the screen glowed bright orange, lit up by the all-consuming cloud. He fired the boosters again—a final desperate blast.

This time the boulders gave way—their bottoms now melted by the engulfing lava. The car slipped through the broken-down dam. The deep lava pool receded, spilling down the road. Through parted rocks, Veronica's dad saw the tunnel beneath Wolf Creek just ahead. He switched off Lava Boat Mode, the lava tires popped out, and he regained normal steering.

"That's the way out, girls!" he said. "Hold your breath!"

The girls looked out at the shapeless cloud of grey death now no more than fifty feet away. This time they knew they would make it. The car accelerated through the tunnel.

Veronica watched the pyroclastic cloud, still furious and hot, shrink ever smaller in the rear window. Someone exhaled loudly. Veronica and Maddy looked at each other and then to Lucky Bunny, who closed her eyes and nestled into Veronica's lap.

The Cloud Forest

CHAPTER 10

Beyond the tunnel, a four-lane highway stretched across a level plain. Veronica's dad checked the rearview mirror for the cloud.

"Well, that was a little close," he said. "Girls, you can use the iPad if you like. We'll be in the Cloud Forest in no time."

Now, on a wide, flat road, Veronica was happy to have something to take her mind off the drive. She and Maddy played on the iPad, building—of all things—their own virtual volcanoes in their favorite app, LavaCraft.

With each passing mile, the world became more normal, the sun brighter, the sky less full of menace, as if the hellish scene unfolding sixty miles to the west had never happened at all. Veronica and Maddy watched the birds land lazily on the wildflowers and chatted about the pearls they hoped to find on the far side of Mount Mystery.

For the first time since the Pass, the lava car slowed, then turned sharply at an unmarked intersection. The smooth highway transformed into bone-crunching dirt road.

Higher and higher the car climbed, bumping along the dusty detour to a ridgeline more than a thousand feet high. Another tunnel marked the end of the road—only this was no normal tunnel. A tree, towering to the heavens, stood in the center of the road. A hole, big enough to fit a tractor-trailer, cut through the bottom of its massive trunk.

Veronica read the sign hanging over the gaping entrance:

HERE STANDS CLOUD FOREST

PLANETARY MONUMENT

SOUL OF DIRT AND SKY

They passed through the primordial tower and parked just on the other side. "Here we are then," Veronica's Dad said. "The trailhead. Everyone out . . . and gear up!"

The Captain opened his door first, stretched his long legs, and groaned loudly in the cool, moist air. He moved stiffly to the back of the car, opened the trunk, and divvied out the backpacks. "You'll be carrying your *own*," he stressed to Maddy, "for the *whole* time!"

Naturally, the Captain's pack was the biggest of them all. Maddy and Veronica traveled light, leaving plenty of room for the pearls they hoped to find along the way. Each girl carried a hammock tent, snacks, sunscreen, rope, a flashlight, bug spray, water, and volcano booties. Veronica had one extra item, a fuzzy one named Lucky Bunny, who fit snugly into a netted pocket.

The four hikers stepped into the stately forest. The waters of a gentle brook murmured into otherwise total silence, marking the trail through the living towers. "This is an ancient redwood grove," narrated the Captain. "Some of these trees are more than two thousand years old."

Veronica looked up, and her mouth fell open.

"Yes," he said, "and they're tall too! In fact, these are the tallest living things on Earth. We'll make camp at a very special place. The natives called it *Chowilawu*, where water bridges earth and sky."

Dim and damp, the Cloud Forest lived up to its name. A chill mist hung in the air, soaking their clothes. The treetops filtered the sun's rays, trapping the forest floor in perpetual twilight. The deadfall of long-rotten trees decayed into the pungent soil. The earth seeped and puddled under their every step.

The Captain continued his lesson: "Each tree drinks more than two thousand cups of water a day. The fog supplies half—the rain the rest. And the roots, they're shallower than you'd think, no more than five feet deep. But they stretch far and wide, intermingling with the roots of their neighbors. Together they stand, sipping from the brook, drinking from the sky, each tree holding up the whole forest."

"Daddy, I'm thirsty," Maddy said, bending down by the brook. She filled her canteen and guzzled it down like a thirsty tree.

Veronica, meanwhile, marveled at the wooden world all around her: at the ferns towering overhead, at the humming-birds standing still in midair, and especially at the red ruddy trunks—some straight, some leaning, some burned, and some hollowed—but all thriving and impossibly tall. She heard the staccato trilling of a woodpecker high overhead, its echo dampened by the moist wood.

"You see these here?" the Captain asked, gesturing to a cluster of trees. "See how they circle this stump? It's a family circle. Before a redwood dies, it sprouts new buds, called burls. New redwoods grow from the old, sharing roots, part of the same eternal family."

Veronica and Maddy weren't listening. They had wandered into the hollow base of one of the gnarled and striated towers. "This one's like a little house," Veronica said, as if walking through the doorway. Inside the tree, Veronica ran her hands across the surface, blackened and smoothed by countless campfires over countless years. She heard a quiet rush, as if standing inside a conch shell. "Why can't we sleep here tonight?" she asked.

"Because that's not the plan," the Captain said. "Now let's go."

The trail veered away from the brook and up a steep canyon wall, narrowing as it veered. Veronica led the single-file line up the trail, with Maddy following close behind. Dense trees and brush scratched at their skin and tore at their clothes as they ducked, hopped, and tripped over the jutting branches and roots.

Some time later, they ascended above the fog. Veronica stopped suddenly in the middle of the trail. In front of her, a band of frogs sunned themselves. The largest stared at Veronica, its ruby red eyes set off by the golden hue of its skin.

Uh-oh, she thought. She knew better than to mess with animals that advertise their colors.

"They're poison dart frogs," said the Captain. "Each one has enough venom to kill twenty men."

Veronica watched the frogs watch her, sensing their wonder at the two-legged creature so out of place in their wood. The frogs took turns hopping lazily then pausing, unburdened by time.

One of the smaller ones bumped the largest. It hopped high, landing directly on Veronica's shoe. A single drop of its venomous skin could have killed her where she stood. But Veronica did not flinch. She imagined the frog imagining her, wondering which was more fearsome. The Captain clapped his hands, half to scare away the frog and half to snap Veronica from her daydream. In either case it worked, and the frog hopped harmlessly away.

"Captain," she said in a tired voice, "it's been all rock and roots for hours. Where's Mount Mystery?"

"Exactly where it's always been," he said, "and where it'll always be. There's a clearing just ahead. You'll be able to see it from there."

Veronica's pace quickened, and she reached the ridgeline first. Due west, white, fluffy clouds stretched before her like a comforter on a cozy bed. Over the clouds, a narrow suspension bridge extended more than a mile to a lush green, small volcano. Behind that, Mount Mystery rose like a colossus out of the deep blue sea.

"You see there," the Captain said. "This is a peninsula.

Mount Mystery is surrounded on three sides by Fire Bay." He pointed south. "On a day like this, you can see clear to New Lava City."

Maddy squinted at the glinting shapes of the skyscrapers across the bay. Compared to Mount Mystery, the metropolis of millions looked like a toy city.

Veronica turned north toward Magma Pass, where angry grey-black clouds still billowed and flashed. She knew, somewhere beyond those clouds, her mother was waiting and worrying. She looked back to the west, her eyes rising up the monstrous volcano's peak.

A gurgling noise, like the rumble of a tummy, but impossibly loud, rolled over them. A single white ring puffed high overhead. The peak flickered orange then ignited, venting its murderous gases high into the heavens. Veronica thought of her mother, her sister, and her beautiful home. She thought of her grandmother, the pearls, and the adventure that awaited.

A Chance Meeting
CHAPTER 11

The high steel bridge crossed a fluffy white sea. "We'll take it over the clouds," the Captain said to the girls. "I was no older than you when I crossed this bridge for the first time. The campsite is just on the other side, down the small volcano. Let's break here and catch our breath, before the final push."

Hungry from the hike, the girls scavenged in their packs. Veronica retrieved a granola bar and Maddy an apple. Together, they rested on some nearby rocks, gazing at scarlet wildflowers as birdsong filled the air.

Veronica heard footsteps. Two hikers approached from the south, a silver-haired man and a blonde-haired boy. The man seemed to be at least seventy years old and the boy no older than twelve.

"Howdee!" yelled the old timer in a thin, high voice. "On the way to Mystery, too?"

"Yes, sir!" the Captain said. "Made our way over Magma Pass. How about you?"

"From New Lava City, thank goodness," the old man said, with a nod to the angry northern sky. "It's my grandson's first time. He has this crazy idea of finding pearls. Kids never change I guess. Me? I'm too old for this. It should be his parents out here. But his father, he never met the boy, and his mother, she lost interest in Mystery years ago. Spends all her time working in some high-rise over yonder, investing in a life she doesn't live."

Set in the shadow of the great volcano, New Lava City was the region's only metropolis. Its wealthy residents competed for the best view, erecting skyscraper after skyscraper, each one higher than the last. But unlike a normal city, its weathermen not only forecasted the rain and snow; they also predicted the ash—and how many inches of it would fall each day.

The great volcano marked every aspect of city life. Huge retractable roofs protected the outdoor shopping centers, and ash plows were a common sight on the avenues in all seasons. By law, all apartment buildings, offices, and stores required the finest HEPA filters. The filters prevented ash-clog in the heating and cooling systems and provided the first line of defense against poisonous gas clouds.

For all the drawbacks of volcanic living, its citizens never tired of boasting. Numerous billboards lined the roads in and out of the city, touting the many benefits of volcanic life:

ASH-FREE 300 DAYS A YEAR!

CHEAP ENERGY = GOOD BUSINESS!

COME FOR THE HOT SPRINGS, STAY FOR THE JOBS!

"How about you fine people?" the old man said. "Where're you from?"

The Captain rolled his eyes. Every city dweller he had ever known praised New Lava City as if it were the center of the universe, as if it were Rome in its heyday—the only right place to live. "Crater Lake," he said.

The old man's face lit up. "You don't say? My favorite place in the world! I'd take the stillness of the lake over the hubbub of the city any day of the week, I'll tell you that."

Veronica studied the boy carefully. He looked to be about her height but with hair as blonde as Elyse's. A slingshot dangled out of one hand; his other hand rummaged in his backpack. She noticed the stitched letters on the front of his pack: DAVID HIDE MOLTEN.

"Your last name is *really* Molten?" Veronica asked, gobsmacked. *Veronica Pearl Molten*, she thought, wishing she had a volcanic last name too.

The boy nodded. He plopped himself down on a large rock and produced a box of crackers.

"Can I have one?" Maddy asked.

He removed a handful and loaded his slingshot. An orange cracker bounced off Maddy's lips and into the dirt. The second one landed in her mouth. She ducked for cover, not sure what to make of the strange boy. But just as quickly, he stopped shooting and passed her the whole box. She took it eagerly.

The old man, meanwhile, wrestled to remove what looked like a green metal lunchbox from the bridge.

"What's that?" the Captain asked.

"What's that?!" the old man teased. "Don't you know? This here's a box of dreams. Wanderers like you and me, we come up here—to the top of the world—and leave our thoughts, our poems, our wishes, our random utterances, for the volcano and future wanderers. Been doing it for ages."

The Captain now noticed eight other canisters attached to the bridge. He could not imagine how, in all his previous trips, he had never noticed them before. "Well," he said red-faced, "maybe we lake folk really are a bunch of bumpkins after all."

The boy helped his grandfather unlatch the container. Scraps of paper blew away on the breeze. The boy raced along the ridge after them, reading each one to himself before returning it to the box. He set aside his three favorites.

"What do they say? Read them to us," Maddy said.

David said nothing.

"Young David here doesn't speak," the old man said. "Not since his brother died."

Maddy chose not to pry. "Then can *you* read them?" she asked.

The old man smoothed the first crumpled note over his knee and read it out loud:

> *Please make my mom well.*
> *Make her sing and dance again.*
> *Are you listening?*

Then he read the second:

> *You are not alone,*
> *You can never be alone,*
> *My blood stains your feet.*

The third was longer, with each line written in a different hiker's hand:

> *Proud cloud forest*
> *Dim, damp wood*
> *How well you must know the sunrise*
> *And listen to the night!*
> *To say you know this place*
> *Is to say you know yourself.*
> *Whisper your secrets to the heavens*
> *Teach us, we lovers of change*
> *How to improve a forest?*
> *Humanity sprouts now*
> *But not forever.*

Maddy giggled. "But a tree can't watch the sunrise," she said. "It doesn't have eyes."

"Young lady!" said the old man, as if offended. "Look around! You think you know more than a tree? Why? Because you can talk? Because you have ears? The redwoods talk to the wind, they listen to the birds, they . . ."

"I-I-I just meant," Maddy stammered, "it's just a tree, and trees can't, you know, *see*."

The boy shook his head. He had heard his grandfather's spiel before.

"And what *just* are you?!" the old man said. "You are here because the sun is here, the Earth is here, the fish are here, the plants are here, the animals are here. You are here because your mother and father and their mothers and fathers who had mothers and fathers are all here, still, in you. You depend on everything and everything depends on you."

He scribbled madly on a scrap of paper, reading as he wrote:

The dead are a gift to the living and the living to the dead. Touch a thousand people and live a thousand lives.

With her own paper, Veronica thought about the old man's words. She thought about her sister, and she thought about the boy. She scrawled on the paper so no one could see, stuffed it in the box, and said: "This is a future letter to me."

Dear Veronica,

Mystery is everywhere. But you have to look :)

Love always,

Veronica

Maddy, meanwhile, said nothing. She did not care at all for the old man's advice or his manner of dispensing it. She scarfed down more crackers and joined the boy, who flipped through a photo book of volcano pearls. Together, they admired the many sizes and colors, hoping they'd find at least *one* somewhere, anywhere, on the mysterious monster looming just beyond.

After a time, the Captain cleared his throat. "Break time is over, girls," he said. "Next stop . . . camp." He turned to the old man. "It was a pleasure meeting you. And I hope to see you again, on this quest or the next. And you—" he added to the boy, "take care of your grandpa, and remember, *safety* before pearls."

"The pleasure was mine," the old man said. "But before you go, know this. And promise me you won't forget it."

Both girls leaned in, as if to receive a secret.

"Now listen," the old man said. "No matter what happens, no matter how many pearls you find, you must remember this one thing: *Leave some for us!*" He laughed, or at least he meant to, but it came out as a deep phlegmy cough.

Veronica's dad and the Captain shook his hand and set off on their way. The old man and the boy sat and snacked, watching the others step onto the bridge and disappear into the distance.

Setting Up Camp

CHAPTER 12

Veronica, Maddy, and their fathers stepped out in single file onto the narrow steel bridge. From her perch, Veronica could see the tops of the highest trees poking through the marshmallow clouds. At the center of the bridge, the clouds parted, revealing a lush green forest below. Towering redwoods gave way to old-growth fig, cedar, and teak.

They continued along the bridge to the small volcano on the other side, emerging onto a mossy glen. A crystal-clear stream meandered through the glen and down the slope. Mount Mystery loomed in the distance.

"We're almost there," the Captain said. "Just follow the stream down, and you'll find the campsite. And don't worry, this volcano's extinct."

Extinct. Veronica had heard that word at least twice before. Once, in science class, describing the ancient volcano at the center of her own hometown, and again, from her father, describing the volcano that would eventually destroy Babeltown.

Together they descended with the stream into the forest, moss drapes deafening every footfall and birdcall. Veronica felt as if the earth itself had stopped rotating, as if everything would always be still and calm and exactly the same.

Maddy broke the silence first, feeling drops of liquid on her hair and shoulders. "Rain," she grumbled. "Just our luck." The drops quickened into a steady spray.

Veronica looked up horrified. "Maddy," she said, "it's not rain. It's . . . it's . . . monkey pee."

Maddy laughed, certain her friend was joking. Suddenly, an enormous rustling filled the canopy. The roar of howler monkeys exploded above their heads. Deep, grave howls echoed off the forest floor. Maddy took off running. Half-crazed, she raced down the trail, her hands covering her ears, paying no attention to the rugged path.

Her foot snagged in the gap between a root and the ground. She hurtled head first toward a jagged rock.

"You must be more careful!" the Captain said, grabbing her pee-soaked arm just in time. "No one can save you out here. There are no ambulances, no hospitals, and besides, you're running from nothing. They're only howlers—noisy, not dangerous. They're just marking their territory."

Maddy caught a whiff of herself and nearly puked with disgust. Her clothes and hair reeked with the acrid stink of monkey pee. In her current condition, she did not care at all to hear a nature lesson from her father. The disturbed howlers continued to roar like a city at rush hour.

The Captain did his best not to laugh. "Don't worry, darling," he consoled. "You can wash off soon. We're nearly there."

But Maddy knew when her father said *nearly* it was never *nearly* close enough. On they walked for another thirty minutes following the stream down the volcano. At the bottom, the trail leveled off and the stream vanished behind a wall of bamboo. The muffled rush of running water beckoned them.

The Captain stepped into the bamboo forest, toward the sound. The others followed. "Close your eyes and keep them closed," the Captain called to the girls. He took them each by the hand and led them carefully and blindly through the thick bamboo. The girls could feel the long thin shoots scratching against their arms and legs until finally they stood in the clear.

"Okay," he said. "Open them! I give you . . . *Chowilawu*."

Here deep in the green wood, a wide, crystal-clear waterfall spilled out of the sky, carving a small but impossibly pale blue pool out of stone. A blaze of purple and pink azaleas, white snowbrush, and red salmonberry formed a flowery hoop around the waters. Fish splashed, dragonflies danced, and salamanders sunned themselves on the rocks. The pool reflected the day like a rippling mirror—an oasis so surreal and so perfect it had to be a dream.

Veronica and Maddy reached down to touch the milky waters. "It's blue," Veronica whispered, cupping the water, "even in my hands!"

The Captain continued: "You see, that clear stream there

flows into the pool and mixes with the clear waterfall to make this pale blue color. That other stream flows out of the pool and carries the milky blue waters all the way to Mount Mystery."

"But I don't get it," Maddy said. "How can a clear waterfall and a clear stream make blue water?"

"There are volcanic minerals in the soil," the Captain said. "The waterfall carries sulfur and the stream brings calcium carbonate. They mix here in this pool, and when they do, the water turns unimaginably blue. But don't worry, it's safe to swim in or drink. *Chowilawu* is a perfect—and perfectly hidden—honey hole."

Veronica studied the stream feeding the chemical-blue pool. "Are you sure it's sa—?"

Splash. Fully clothed and stinking of monkey pee, Maddy jumped off the nearest rock. The others watched her head vanish, then pop up again behind the waterfall's wispy veil. "Come in!" she yelled.

Veronica stripped to her bathing suit and clambered up a high rock on the side of the pool. "How deep is it?" she asked.

"Deep enough!" Maddy said. "NOW JUMP!"

And jump Veronica did, without even holding her nose. Her feet plunged into the milk-blue waters, never finding the bottom. "There's fish everywhere," she yelled as she surfaced. "You don't even need worms!"

The girls swam and splashed in the fairy-tale waters, making the most of the remaining daylight. They explored the curious boundary where clear and clear made blue, and Veronica even managed to barehand a fish.

Naturally, she threw it at her friend, but Maddy saw it coming. She tilted her head, just in time, to sniff the fish and watch it fly past her nose. The fish swam excitedly away.

The dads busied themselves setting up camp. Veronica's dad dug for worms and fished for dinner, while the Captain hung the hammocks. Lucky Bunny hopped daintily to the pool's edge, cleaning her paws and sipping at the blue waters. The sun slipped behind the trees, and dusk fell upon the forest.

"Come out, girls!" the Captain called. "It's getting late . . . and there's work to be done."

The girls listened, leaving the warm blue waters for the chill forest air. Dotted with goosebumps, they picked their way through the rocks to the campsite. Maddy's eyes drifted up to the trees. "Bunk hammocks!" she said.

All four hammocks were strung between two trees like bunk beds. Veronica's hammock was on top, at least forty feet high, with Maddy's hammock just beneath it. The first tree was perfect for climbing, with small branches poking out of the trunk like a ladder.

"Why so high?" Maddy asked.

"Animals," said the Captain. "Big ones."

"How big?"

"It doesn't matter," he said. "They're not the problem. The dark is. We need firewood. Why don't you two go see if you can find some?" As he spoke, he piled rocks into a makeshift fire pit across from the hammocks.

Maddy nodded. "If we find some, can we have s'mores?"

"Absolutely not," the Captain said. "Tomorrow is the most

important hike of your life. We're not about to get all sugared up the night before. You need a good night's rest. We all do."

Maddy's shoulders slouched, and Veronica's face drooped. Together they plodded out of the campsite in search of wood, shuffling their feet, their bellies growling for marshmallows.

Veronica's dad rummaged in his pack. "Oh, would you look at that?" he said loudly. "Here's some marshmallows. Graham crackers and chocolate too. S'mores for everyone!"

The Captain huffed, as the girls now skipped into the forest. Deeper and deeper they went, searching for dry wood amidst the cool dampness and thinking only of s'mores and mystery. Fireflies blinked on and off all around them. The dark came fast.

The Torch

CHAPTER 13

Veronica's dad reeled in another good-sized trout from the pale blue waters. He called for the girls, but they did not answer.

"Hey Captain," he said. "Have you seen them?"

The Captain looked around, checked his watch, then stared into the not-quite dark. "They could be anywhere."

"Veronica! Maddy! Veronica! Maddy!" the two fathers called in every direction. "VERONICA! MADDY!"

But Veronica and Maddy could not hear their fathers' cries. The girls walked deeper into the forest. Somewhere in the distance, a wild animal howled.

"Hey, Maddy," Veronica said, her hands full of firewood. "Which way is camp?"

"Umm . . . right over . . . there?" She pointed uncertainly. Every direction looked exactly the same. She listened for the rush of the waterfall but heard only more howls, now closer than before.

"It has to be somewhere," she said. "We didn't go that far, did we?" She peered through the trunks for any movement, any light, any sign of the campsite at all. "There!" she shouted. "The light! That's it!"

They hurried toward the light, which brightened as they neared. "Dad, we're coming!" they yelled. "We're coming! We're over here!"

The girls pressed through a thicket of wild plum trees and found the light.

"FIRE!" yelled Maddy. "RUN!"

But Veronica did not run. She blinked her eyes and moved closer. "It's not fire, Maddy. It's . . . fireflies!"

The burning bush just in front of them glowed pale yellow, twinkling like the night sky. Mounds of fireflies piled on every leaf. A fine dust sparkled the ground, fireflies coating every speck.

Maddy moved closer. She stooped down to run her fingers through it. "It's pollen," she said. "The fireflies are attracted to the pollen."

Veronica noticed how the bush flickered in spots and in others shone solidly. She inspected further. "When one blinks off, dozens more are blinking on behind it," she said.

"That's it!" Maddy said. "Hold this!" She handed all of her firewood to Veronica, except for one large log. Maddy rolled the top of it in the pollen, then held it to the bush. Beams of fireflies radiated toward it like a force field. The top of the log dimly flickered, brightened, and then glowed constant. Her firefly torch illuminated the dark wood.

Back at the camp, the fathers, now desperate, continued shouting for their daughters. Veronica's dad climbed up the hammock tree, flashlight in hand. From a high branch, he pointed his beam in all directions.

"Do you see them?" asked the Captain.

Veronica's dad didn't answer.

"Well, do you see them or not?" the Captain repeated.

"I see something . . . a light far away," Veronica's dad said. "But it can't be them. They didn't take their flashlights. It's probably just the old man and the boy, making camp somewhere."

Even in the dense forest the girls noticed the high white light in the distance. They wanted to run but couldn't. The ground was too treacherous and Veronica's arms too full of wood. They picked their way slowly through the forest toward the light.

Veronica's father peered out from the treetop. "It's getting brighter," he said. "Somebody's out there . . . MADDY . . . VERONICA . . . IS THAT YOU?"

The high-pitched squeal of two young girls—no longer lost in the woods—echoed through the forest. Veronica's dad grinned from ear to ear.

The Captain frowned, slumping against a tree. Though he was relieved, the enormity of the trip's danger dawned on him. Now was the time, he reasoned, to put an end to this once and for all, before anyone got hurt, or worse, *killed*. If he couldn't protect them at a campsite, what hope did he have of keeping them safe on Mount Mystery tomorrow?

He steeled himself for the words he had to say: *that the trip was over, that they must go home first thing in the morning, that Mount Mystery would always be there, but that it would just have to wait—until they were older.*

And then he saw their faces, flickering in the pale yellow light. Maddy held her strange torch high with two hands, while Veronica struggled with a pile of logs.

He ran toward them. "Girls! Where were you? And what's this?"

"It's a firefly torch, Dad," Maddy said. "I made it myself."

Open-mouthed, the Captain examined the torch. He had seen many things but never this. His own daughter had made light out of the night when she needed it most. *What else could she do?* he wondered. He pulled her close and hugged her tight— and decided not to disappoint her.

Veronica's dad slid down the tree, yelling in a singsong voice: "It's s'more time! It's ss'mmoorree time! It's sss'mmmooorr-reee tiiimmmeee!"

Veronica dumped her wood into the fire pit with a heavy thud. The Captain rubbed two sticks together to start the fire, but Veronica's dad beat him to it. He struck a match and sparked the kindling. The fire flickered, then roared to life. He cooked his freshly caught trout over the flame, seasoning it with wild basil.

Warmed by fire, the four hungry hikers gobbled up every bite. "I can't believe just this morning we were home," Veronica said. "Now look at us, sitting around a fire next to a waterfall in the middle of the Cloud Forest. We explored a grave, survived the cave, found a bunny, and escaped Magma Pass. We saw the world's biggest trees, its most poisonous frogs, and its loudest monkeys."

"Enough about the monkeys!" Maddy said. "If I ever see another monkey . . . I swear I'll . . ."

"There, there," Veronica's dad said. "Now, what do you say we eat the world's most delicious s'mores?" He handed out marshmallows, sticks, graham crackers, and bars of chocolate. The four adventurers leaned into the crackling fire. The flames licked their marshmallows.

"Who knows a ghost story?" Maddy mumbled, her mouth full of marshmallows.

"No ghost stories!" said the Captain. "No nightmares—not tonight. You need your rest."

"But, I'm not sleepy!" Maddy said. "And I *need* a story to fall asleep."

"Oh you *need* one, do you?" the Captain said. "Well, I know something better than a ghost story. It's true and it's old and it's the story of these woods. You see, the trails we walked today, they didn't cut themselves. An ancient people did—the People of Wood."

The People of Wood
CHAPTER 14

The bone-white eye of a low-slung moon stared the Captain in the face. He held the flickering torch close. Maddy and Veronica leaned in, the firefly light dancing in their eyes. He began:

It was a land of dragons and redwoods, of towering ferns and boulder-sized diamonds. The People of Wood filled the cosmos. Their starships filled the universe, and they landed right here in the Cloud Forest.

They roamed the forests for thousands of years with no concept of *private property* or even of *my*. They lived as naked as they were born, and as naked as they would die. Everything and nothing was theirs.

They believed in the dream force: the reality that lies behind all things, a world they could touch only in their dreams. They believed everything you see—the entire observable universe—was a mere shadow of a dream.

They believed there were those among them—the Dreamers—who dreamt, even while awake. They believed space and time bent to these Dreamers, that the whole universe existed simply to make their dreams come true, that every Dreamer dreamt a different part of the same beautiful dream.

They lived the way their grandfather's grandfathers lived, and they lived that way for thousands of years. No people anywhere lived in one place longer than the People of Wood lived here.

"But—that's not true," Veronica said. "That's not what we learned in school. The natives weren't good; they were savages! And Captain John the First fought them. That's what really happened."

"Oh, is that what *really* happened?" the Captain said. "Not everything makes it into the history books, Veronica, not most things even, and not these things for sure. Some people don't write the histories. I know what I know because Captain John the First was a friend of the last Dreamer. They died together at the hands of the Diamond King, a man you don't believe existed. But every time I tell this tale I fulfill my great-great-great . . . grandfather's dying wish: to never let the world forget the People of Wood."

"But the statue in town . . ." Veronica said breathlessly. "It's just Captain John all by himself. He died fighting natives. And *you* of all people should know that."

"Legends change, Veronica," the Captain said. "Back then, there were no photographs, no videotapes, just stories told and retold. Captain John lost. He died. His enemies wrote the history. Captain John the First is a hero because they made him one."

"Who made him one?" she said. "What are you talking about? What *really* happened?"

A smile curled on his lips, and he leaned in to the fire:

I'll tell you what happened: the Diamond King. The People of Wood had more diamonds than you could ever imagine. Back then, diamonds were like blades of grass, uncountable and everywhere. In those days, even the volcanoes erupted diamonds.

The People of Wood built their lives around the diamonds and the diamonds around their lives. They used diamond blocks to construct their homes, diamond sheets to cook their food, and diamond arrowheads to hunt for dragons, their primary food.

Diamonds were so much a part of their lives that they made them a part of their deaths as well. Just as we have funerals to bury our dead, the People of Wood had their own sacred rites.

They would lay their dead in a canoe carved from a single cinnamon tree. Each tribesman would place a single diamond into the canoe, until it overflowed with gems of every hue—clear, blue, red, green, purple, even black. Then, they'd launch the boat downriver and give their loved one back to the forest. Now, no

one knows if the Diamond King came looking for diamonds or merely happened upon them, but one thing is certain. He found a canoe laden with diamonds, pulled it to shore, and fashioned himself a crown from the dazzling stones.

He poled himself upstream. There, he discovered the People of Wood. They greeted him like a brother, but he insisted he was their king.

"What's a king?" they laughed. But they did not laugh for long. You see, the Diamond King was not like them. He wanted only to possess the world and to give nothing. He was empty to the depths of his soul, and he filled that emptiness with diamonds. He would sooner destroy the world than share it.

So what did he do? He left the forest and returned to Crater Lake, where settlers had arrived from a faraway shore. He promised them riches beyond their wildest dreams, if only they paid the price: the blood of an ancient people, a *primitive people*, he said, who worshipped the devil.

The settlers promised peace in return for diamonds. They signed treaties to last as long as the diamonds glittered and the sun rose. The People of Wood had no fear. They shared everything: every diamond vein, every hidden mine. To them, hiding a diamond was as strange as hiding the sun.

The People of Wood were strong and many. They hunted dragons with their third eye, their dream force. But they never hunted each other. The earth was their church. They could not kill a dragon without a word of thanks, nor drink from a stream without a song of praise.

When the Diamond King knew everything there was to know—after he mapped their land and counted their numbers—he attacked them sleeping in the dead of night. He burned the forests, murdered the women, and drove the children into the night. The People of Wood shared everything, and he slaughtered them for it, like buffalo in the field.

On that fateful day, the last day of their lives, Captain John and the Dreamer set out to stop the Diamond King. But it was too late, and the Diamond King too clever.

You see, he had his own third eye, his own dream force, a way to make *his* nightmares come true. And he was ready for them. He set his trap, and he murdered them both.

The time for fighting had passed. The time for mourning had come.

But before he set out on that last journey, Captain John hid away his young son. He gave him one instruction: to never let the world forget the People of Wood. According to legend, the boy hid in the caves of Babeltown. He didn't fight that day, and that is why I am here, sixteen generations later, telling you this story.

Veronica's dad chuckled and slapped his knee. "Quite the tall tale, John!" he said.

"Tall tale?" sneered the Captain. "Then what do you call this?" In one motion, he pulled his shirt over his head, revealing an enormous tattoo. Zigzagging lines crisscrossed his entire back like a spider web. Two small triangles marked the tattoo's upper corners.

The Captain continued: "The night before his death, the Dreamer tattooed this mark on the Captain's son's back. No one knew what it meant, and I still don't. But every Captain John since has received this tattoo on his eighteenth birthday, applied in the tribal style, with bone chisel and burnt-wood ink, just as it was five hundred years ago. The only thing left of that proud people is my story and this mark."

"You mean, they died?" Maddy said, dumbfounded. "All of them?"

"Well . . . not exactly," said the Captain. "Every now and then, you'll catch a glimpse of their last boat in Fire Bay—the *Dragon Prau*—its red sails billowing in the wind. They used to live everywhere and nowhere, roaming the forests like dolphins roam the ocean. Now, they make their home in the one place no one ever took from them: Dragon Island. It's far to the south through rough seas.

"From time to time, you'll see them in New Lava City, trading carvings for medicine. *But stay away.* They're not the People of Wood, not anymore. They're killers now, and worse—cannibals, people who eat people. Once they had mountains of diamonds, now they have nothing, not even their souls. They're the sea-wandering pirates of Dragon Island, and if you get too close, they'll eat you up!"

Veronica shivered. "Could he come back?" she asked. "Could it happen again?"

"Of course it could happen again," the Captain said. "The Diamond King may be dead, but there's always another madman, making mad plans. Read your history. Every terrible thing has happened. And every terrible thing will happen again, no matter how many cell phones we have, no matter how smart we think we are, no matter how sure we are this time it's different. When good people become afraid, they become the very people they fear the most."

Veronica remembered Babeltown and the story of its last days: the break-ins, the looting, the hunger. "But good always wins in the end, doesn't it?" she asked.

"No," said the Captain, "it doesn't. Good only wins when enough good people stand up to make sure that it does."

Veronica thought again of the blind jeweler's warning, that an evil was coming and coming in white. She wished he was just a foolish old man, but somehow she knew better. *If an evil did come*, she wondered, *would she stand up to stop it?*

Veronica's father had heard enough of the Captain's tall tale. He could see that his daughter was hanging on every far-fetched word. "Captain," he said, "tell us. Where are all the diamonds?"

"Ahhh, yes," the Captain sighed. "Now that's the trillion-dollar question. The diamonds vanished, along with the Diamond King."

Veronica shook her head. "But how can you hide that many diamonds?"

"You *can't*, Veronica!" her dad thundered. "Don't you see? The story is pure hogwash. I'm sure the Captain's family has been telling it around campfires for generations, but that doesn't make it true." Still, he was surprised, and a little impressed, that someone as straitlaced as the Captain had such a big tattoo.

"Well, I believe my dad!" Maddy said.

Veronica didn't know what to believe. "All I know," she said, "is I wish I could have lived back then."

"*Back then!*" her father said, his voice a pitch too high. "Why would you ever want to live back then?"

"Because there was mystery!" Veronica said. "People crossed oceans! Fought pirates! Slew dragons! Now, if I want to know something, I just search for it on the iPad. There's nothing left to discover."

Her father looked up at the star-dusted sky. "Oh, everything is known then, is it?" he said. "Look up, Veronica. I believe there are creatures up there—creatures we haven't found yet—looking back at us right now. Imagine such a creature. She's standing on a planet, spinning around a fireball that is her day.

"To her, our earth, our home, our entire world, is just another pale blue dot suspended in the vastness of space, like every other dot, a twinkling pixel in the galaxy, itself a pixel in the universe. She's up there right now, Veronica, wrapped in a starry night, looking up, and asking herself the same question as you: *Is anyone looking back?*

"But mystery is not just up there, it's everywhere. We could be in a black hole right now in someone else's universe. Or we could be holograms, dancing in the shadows of a deeper reality. We don't know why there's space, why there's time, or why we're here . . ."

Veronica yawned. "I know why we're here," she said. "We're here to climb Mount Mystery in the morning."

With that, Veronica and Lucky Bunny climbed into their high hammock. Maddy followed. They zipped the bug nets over their bodies and heard everything: the snap of a branch, the wail of a bobcat.

Veronica gazed into the milky center of the galaxy. A shooting star streaked overhead, then another and another. Veronica never felt so small, or so much a part of the universe.

The girls fell asleep.

The Cinnamon Forest
CHAPTER 15

"No! Help!" Veronica cried, thrashing her arms and legs. "Mom! Dad!! Elyse!!!"

She awoke, expecting to find herself forty feet high near one of the most dangerous volcanoes on earth, but her pillow was too fluffy and her blanket too warm. She could hear her sister Elyse snoring somewhere nearby.

"Oh, thank goodness," she sighed. "It was only a dream." She pulled the soft blanket over her head, but something sharp poked her in the back. Her heavy eyes opened to a haze of white moongleam.

"Veronica, wake up! It's time to go," the voice was familiar but faraway. Her eyes widened, and she saw herself as she was, dangling in the trees of a cool summer night, the pearl fields of Mount Mystery a day's walk away. "Which is real?" she croaked.

"Sleepyhead, we have to GO!" Maddy repeated, poking her again with a marshmallow stick.

"I think . . . I think . . . I had a bad dream," Veronica said.

"Yeah, you think?" Maddy said plainly. "I've been trying to wake you. What happened?"

"I—thought—it—was—real," Veronica said. "I was standing in the dark over a fiery pit. I tried to yell, but no words came out. All I could here were voices, voices I knew, chanting in the night: 'SACRIFICE, SACRIFICE, SACRIFICE!' Everything went white. A hand pressed my back. It was the Diamond King. He pushed me, and I fell."

"Daaa—aaa—aad!" Maddy called in a singsong voice. "The Diamond King gave Veronica a nightmare."

The Captain hoped he'd heard her wrong. "What did you say?"

"You know, your story from last night," she said again. "It gave Veronica a nightmare."

"Did you see his face?" he said.

"What? Why?" said Veronica. "Does it mean something?"

"No, dreams mean nothing," the Captain lied. But he had heard of other stories, other visions of the Diamond King in the Cloud Forest. And no one had ever seen his face. What's more, something terrible always happened to the dreamer— and not just in the dream. As a boy, around a campfire, the Captain learned the curse of the Cloud Forest, that a dream of the Diamond King there was more than a dream—it was a looking glass. *She would be dead soon*, he thought.

He laughed at himself. *What a silly superstition. Dreams don't matter.* Unsure what to make of it, he made nothing of it at all. "Let's go," he said.

It was five o'clock in the morning, and the blue light of false dawn bathed the forest in an eerie glow. The four adventurers climbed down from the trees, packed up their things, and grabbed their hiking sticks.

They set out at a brisk pace through the predawn dark. Suddenly, the trees changed, and the pungent aroma of cinnamon cider filled their nostrils. A spicy paradise enveloped them.

"Girls, this is the Cinnamon Forest," the Captain explained. "Every tree you see is cinnamon, nutmeg, or clove. You'll know the cinnamon by its smell, the nutmeg by its yellow flower, and the clove by its pink-brown fruit."

Maddy could not resist the clove. She picked one and bit into it. A bitter sweetness flooded her mouth. Her eyes watered, and her tongue went numb. "Dath, canth we thop for a jink?" she managed.

"There's a clearing just over the hill," he said, pointing. "We'll stop there." The puffy-eyed hikers shared yawns and continued up the hill. They could hear the popping and cracking of rock, like gunfire in the distance.

Suddenly, the trees cleared, and Mount Mystery burst into view. Blue lava rivers blazed down the volcano like surreal sapphire fingers, spilling into a deep gorge just out of sight. A steel-blue fountain illuminated the peak.

Veronica could not believe her eyes. "Mount Mystery has blue lava!" she exclaimed.

"It only looks blue at night," her father said. "Mount Mystery erupts sulfur. Sulfur is yellow, but it burns blue. What you see is the steel-blue flame of molten sulfur." He pointed to a boulder pile. "This is as good a place as any," he said. "Let's break here."

Maddy slurped from her canteen, gargling and rinsing the bitter clove from her mouth. The others took off their packs and rested on the rocks. Veronica sniffed in the cinnamon aroma and thought of her mother's candles.

Veronica looked up at the volcano. *How can anyone climb that?* she wondered. She distracted herself by drawing with her hiking stick in the soft dirt. She sketched herself climbing up Mount Mystery toward a giant pearl at the top.

On finishing her masterpiece, she stuck her stick between two rocks. "Hey Maddy, look at this," she said, proudly.

Maddy had the canteen to her lips. She spit out her water, spraying her dad. "Veronica!" she yelled. "Your stick is on fire!"

Veronica looked down. Sure enough, flames engulfed the bottom of her hiking stick. She yanked it from between the rocks and smothered it in the dirt, ruining her drawing.

"Yes, umm, please do mind the ground," the Captain said. "The earth's crust can be thin around here—in some places very. Test the ground with your sticks so you don't fall through."

Maddy yawned. *It was too early in the morning to worry about falling through the earth*, she thought.

The clamor of sparrows in the gloss of the nutmeg leaves called the Captain to action. "Daybreak is coming," he said. "We have to move."

They rose and walked in single file through the pungent forest. The sun cracked the horizon. Great wafts of smoke billowed from the peak.

"Not good," the Captain said. "The summit's off limits. We'll have to go around."

"But what about the pearls?" Veronica asked.

"The pearls are said to be in two places," her father said, "at the crater at the top and in the sands of the far side. We can still make it to the far side. We just have to go around."

Veronica calculated that her chances of finding pearls had just been cut in half. "But we came for pearls," she said. "Remember? For mom!"

"That's enough," her father said. "The Captain is right. We can't risk our lives when we can see, plain as day, just how dangerous . . ."

He stopped. He had just stepped past the last tree of the Cinnamon Forest. Behind him a spicy grove grew out of the warm earth. In front of him and across a deep ravine lay a moonscape pocked with craters the size of school buses. Here the earth pulsed with power: geysers steamed, mud pots boiled, and stones smoked like ghosts in the spectral fog.

In front of them, white limestones stepped down the ravine—each an infinity-edged pool of pale blue, boiling water. The water flowed step by widening step into the ravine below. It could have been the stairway to heaven, if it weren't the stairway to hell.

"Grab your volcano booties, girls," the Captain said. "That water looks hot."

Yellow Lake

CHAPTER 16

A top the boiling staircase, Veronica removed the green volcano booties from her pack. "I'm *so* glad to get these out of here," she said. "They're *so* heavy."

She slipped them on over her sneakers. When Veronica chose a color, she always chose green—never pink, never red, but sometimes blue, if there were no green. Maddy felt the same way, except about blue, and she pulled on her blue booties to just above her knee. This time, Maddy filled the empty spot in her backpack with Lucky Bunny, whose face peeked sweetly out one side.

"You know how these work, right girls?" the Captain said. "You can't just go walking around on lava. Your feet would catch fire in seconds. The booties protect you up to three hundred degrees, but lava can be two thousand degrees. Understood?"

The girls nodded their still sleepy heads in unison.

"Good. Now follow me."

The Captain tested the first stair. He poked his hiking stick into the boiling water and tapped the bottom three times. Finding it firm, he stepped down. The water rolled and bubbled around his feet. He repeated the process on each stair. The girls followed, trailed by Veronica's dad.

Step by step, they descended the limestone staircase toward the ravine. A pair of redheaded vultures circled high overhead. "I hope they're not here for us," Maddy said.

Midway, the staircase steepened, and the ravine's bottom burst into view. A narrow, mustard-yellow lake stretched to the horizon in both directions. Beyond the lake, Mount Mystery loomed above them, vast and desolate.

The stink of rotten eggs enveloped them. "That's Yellow Lake," Veronica's dad said. "The bottom is solid sulfur. And I've never seen it so high—or so full. The last time I was here . . . it was dry."

"Is there a bridge?" Maddy asked.

"No, no bridge, and look," the Captain said, pointing, "we've got company." A family of four lizards, each more than ten feet long, sunned themselves on the banks of the yellow waters. "They're Komodo dragons," he said.

Veronica had assumed the dragons from the Captain's campfire story were fake, of the fire-breathing variety, like something out of a cartoon—not Komodo, not real. *What else was real?* she wondered. *What about the People of Wood? What about the diamonds?*

A shriek in the sky drew her eye. The vultures swooped, screeching for blood. She covered her head, as if there were

cover to be had standing helplessly exposed in a puddle of boiling water on the edge of the most monstrous volcano on Earth. Veronica's father waved his hands wildly, shooing the birds away like so many pesky flies. The Captain stood still, certain they were not for them—at least not yet.

The vultures soared past the girls and landed atop the dragons. But the dragons did not flinch.

"They're dead," Maddy gasped. "They're already dead." The vultures tore into the dragons like drumsticks of fried chicken, pecking and tearing, pecking and tearing for what felt like hours but could only have been minutes. Finally, the great birds raised their wings, stepped forward, and fell over—dead.

"Up the stairs!" the Captain yelled. "Now!"

The four adventurers raced back for the Cinnamon Forest and the protection of the trees.

"What happened?" panted Veronica. "What killed the vultures? What killed the dragons?"

"Poison gas," her dad guessed. "Invisible. Probably sulfuric acid, bubbling out of the lake. But I have an idea . . . I know how to clear it." He retrieved a flare from his pack and returned by himself down the limestone stairs, standing in the place he had just fled, one hundred feet above the dead dragons and vultures. He aimed the tube at Yellow Lake and fired.

The flare streaked out of the tube and exploded into the ravine. A great fireball raced up and down the yellow channel. Veronica's father turned to run, but he stumbled forward with the force of the blast. His left hand plunged into one of the pools, as if into a boiling tea kettle. He groaned, picked himself up, and ran for the trees. The others ran to him. "I'm okay, I'm okay," he muttered, wincing, as the others doused canteen water on his burns.

The Captain retrieved burn lotion from his pack. "Well, you don't look okay," he said. "You look like you just got blown up."

Behind him, the flames roared, subsided, and then vanished. Whatever gas had clung to the bottom of the ravine burned off in the violence of the racing fireball.

Deep in thought, Maddy looked out at Yellow Lake. "Of course!" she exclaimed. "The cinnamon trees! Daddy, you can make a raft!"

The Captain smiled at his resourceful daughter. "A cinnamon raft, eh?" he said. "Just like the People of Wood. We can give it a try, but we'll need to tie the logs. I don't have enough rope. See if you girls can find some vines."

The Captain foraged for ten dead cinnamon trees, each between eight and twelve feet tall. He lined them up, then placed two smaller logs across each end. The girls found him vines, and he lashed together a simple log raft.

The Captain turned to Veronica's dad, who was still nursing his hand. "Help me drag this down," he said. "Girls, stay here until we call." The men tied a long vine to each end of the raft, then dragged it clumsily behind them, one step at a time, until they reached the middle stair.

The Captain sniffed deeply for the faintest trace of gas but smelled only the barbecued flesh of blackened vultures and the revolting stink of rotten eggs. "I think it's safe," he said, satisfied. "We're going down." And they pulled the raft to the edge of the yellow water.

"Girls, come now," the Captain called. "And be careful!"

The girls used their sticks to test the solidity of each stair, just as the Captain had showed them. At the bottom, the bubbling yellow water slowly poisoned them, and they knew it. The stench overwhelmed them.

"Maddy and I will go first," the Captain said, climbing onto the raft. He handed Veronica's dad one of the two vines. "Pull the raft back with this after we cross," he told him. "But first you have to push. Push us as hard as you can, but don't get splashed. This isn't yellow water; it's sulfuric acid, a weak one, but strong enough to melt the skin right off your bones."

Veronica and her dad gave the raft a running push. They started from the shore and stepped into the lake up to their knees, just below the tops of their volcano booties. Slowly but surely the cinnamon raft drifted across the acid lake.

Maddy and the Captain stepped off safely onto the base of Mount Mystery. From the opposite shore, Veronica's dad used the second vine to pull the raft back to him and Veronica.

"Okay," the Captain shouted from across the lake. "Now get on!"

Veronica and her dad climbed onto the raft. The Captain and Maddy pulled them hand over hand across the reeking yellow chasm. Veronica coughed, then held her nose. "Daddy," she said nasally, "my nose is burning."

Her dad said nothing. More yellow bubbles rose and popped, like overstretched balloons bursting hundreds of

times a second, poisoning the air bit by bit. The raft floated across the lake.

Together at last, at the base of Mount Mystery, the four adventurers scanned their surroundings. The bubbling, crater-strewn wasteland seemed more like a moon of Jupiter than a mountain of Earth. Now, they had a choice: to go around or to go over the top. The trail around ran parallel to Yellow Lake. It was flat, easy, and long.

And Veronica's dad was certain it would kill them. "I don't know about you, Captain," he said. "But I'd rather not end up like one of those vultures. We either go over the top, or we go home."

The Captain's eyes traveled up the angry volcanic peak—only it was no longer angry. The predawn light show had given way to early morning quiet. He searched for a sign, for any reason to flee, for any excuse to recross Yellow Lake and go home safe and sound.

But Mount Mystery was calm—no smoke, no lava bombs—just perfect, ominous calm. They had come this far, and now, here was the red carpet, rolled out before them. The pearls of the far side lay just ahead: straight over the top.

Glittering Geyser

CHAPTER 17

Knee-deep in ash, Veronica took her first clumsy steps up the volcano. But for every three steps forward, she slid two steps back.

"I'll tie a safety rope to all of us, just in case," the Captain said. He tied one end to himself and connected the other through the belt loops of his fellow adventurers, leaving a few feet between each of them. "There, now at least no one can slide down the volcano," he said.

"Yeah, unless we *all* do," Maddy said.

The Captain and Veronica's dad led the way, their larger steps propelling the girls forward. The steep slope and bulky booties made the hiking slow and sweaty, but they counted themselves lucky for what there wasn't: no lava bombs, no active lava flows, and no earthquakes.

Two hours into the hike, Mount Mystery still towered over them. "The bottom is closer than the top," Veronica complained. "We'll never make it at this rate."

"It's only eight thirty in the morning," the Captain said. "We'll be at the halfway point in an hour. By noon, we'll make the top, with plenty of time to find your pearls."

They pressed on, the war-zone landscape smoking and steaming, increasing in difficulty with each step. Sidestepping between a boiling mud pot and a deep crevice, Veronica slipped. Her dad reached for her but missed, stumbling forward onto his belly. Maddy fell with him, pulled down by the rope tied to her waist.

The Captain planted his feet like anchors. He tugged mightily on the rope. Gritting his teeth, he strained against the combined body weight of three people. "Next time I'm only tying the girls to me," he muttered.

He leaned all his weight up the volcano, managing to slow then stop their fall. The others untangled themselves and stood up, brushing the hot sands from their skin and clothes.

Shaken, they continued their trek, if a bit slower than before. The ashy landscape transformed into a surreal color show. Pools of red, blue, and violet extended in widening circles, and in the center, a geyser erupted like a gigantic fountain, its steaming waters undulating with the rhythms of the deep earth.

The Captain blinked the sweat out of his eyes. "This is the halfway point, ladies," he said. "Last chance to rest before the top." He grunted, slipping the heavy pack off his back. The others joined him. They unfastened the rope from their belts and took off their packs, gulping down water with enormous swallows.

Mesmerized by the dancing fountain, Veronica approached its edge, close enough to toss in a coin and make a wish. All at once, the geyser waters sputtered and then stopped completely, as if someone had flipped a switch. She thought she heard a sound in the distance, something like glass breaking.

The noise grew louder, ringing and clanging. She understood too late what she heard. Deep beneath the earth something hard was ricocheting off the geyser walls and rattling its way to the surface.

Veronica looked up. The last thing she saw was her father running toward her. Then she felt it. The geyser exploded behind her, pelting her with burning rocks. She covered her head and dropped to the ground. The geyser puffed and plumed in a great, glittery cloud.

And then it quieted. Searing hot rocks tumbled from her hair, blistering her skin. She looked again for her father, expecting to be scooped up and saved. But he never came. She saw him stopped dead in his tracks, his mouth wide with wonder.

Her knees knocked as she straightened to standing. She seemed okay enough, all things considered, but her feet would not move. Looking down, she understood why; diamonds buried her legs to the knees and studded her hair. She squinted in the glittering light, dusting the dazzling crystals from her body. "I'd say we found your diamonds, Captain," she said. And she burst into tears.

Her father rushed to her. He dug her feet out of the diamond pile and checked her for burns. The Captain and Maddy joined them at the geyser's edge, peering into the abyss.

Maddy pointed down the geyser hole. "What's that?" she said. Ten feet beneath the surface, she saw twin holes in the geyser wall, as if the geyser cut straight through a tunnel.

"It's just a lava tube," the Captain explained. "Lava tubes are like underground pipes. Rivers of lava flow down the volcano. The top gets exposed to the air and cools first, forming a hard rock ceiling. The lava underneath continues to flow, eventually emptying, and creating a long, hollow tunnel."

"Yes," Veronica's dad said, "and this tube has a geyser cutting right through it." He retrieved his iPad from his backpack. "Fortunately, I should be able to see where it goes. Mount Mystery is covered with sensors, so the ground maps should be accurate." He tapped a button on the screen and located himself. "Yep," he said, "the tube's empty . . . and would you look at that . . . it stretches clear off the screen, all the way to the Cinnamon Forest."

Veronica's eyes twinkled. "Can we explore it?" she asked.

"Veronica Pearl!" her father chided. "There will be no more dumb decisions, no more stupid risks, and there's no way I'm letting you into that tunnel."

The Captain cleared his throat. "All good points," he said, as if Veronica's dad were talking to him. "But these are the first diamonds found on Mount Mystery since Captain John the First. I have to go." He strapped a headlamp to his forehead and removed a rope from his pack.

"Then I'm coming too," Maddy said.

The Captain paused. Here was his daughter, inventor of firefly torches and cinnamon rafts. She shared his blood, his history, and his resourcefulness. "Of course you can come," he said. He tied one end of the rope to a fallen lava bomb the size of a car, and tied the other around his waist. Maddy wrapped her arms and legs around him, and together, they rappelled ten feet down the geyser hole to the tunnel below.

"I think we'll sit this one out," Veronica's dad said. He and Veronica watched from the surface. Veronica's dad checked the iPad. He zoomed in on a scan of Mount Mystery's magma chamber. The last time he had checked, back at the house, everything looked normal. Now, it looked anything but.

He pointed at the screen. "Veronica, look here. You see this bulge on the far side? Just two days ago that wasn't there. And . . . the top crater . . . it rose fifty feet in just twenty-four hours. The pressure is building. The lava wants out."

Veronica laughed. "Then don't go blowing up any more lakes," she teased, as if the very concept of Mount Mystery erupting while she was standing on it was unthinkable.

Down in the lava tube, the Captain mostly saw what he expected. Clear lines on the tube's sides marked the height of previous lava flows. Sharp lavacicles jutted from the tube's ceiling and pink tendrils glowed in the dark along the cave walls. He untied the rope from his waist and explored deeper.

Maddy touched one of the sparkling pink blotches. "Yuck," she groaned. The pink, warm goo clung to her hand, stretching like taffy. She jerked her hand away. "What *is* this stuff?"

"It's tube slime," the Captain said. "It won't hurt you. And it might even help. The same bacteria that's in antibiotics is in that slime, but I wouldn't eat it if I were you."

Maddy had no intention of eating the slime. She followed her dad deeper into the tube, her headlamp darting this way

and that. Then she paused, beaming her light straight down. "Hey, Dad," she said, quizzically. "What's with these lines?"

The Captain dropped to his knees. He ran his fingers down two parallel grooves that extended as far as he could see. His hands, so steady, began to shake. His eyes, so sharp, blurred with tears. "That's it!" he said. "The secret!"

The Crater

CHAPTER 18

The Captain hid his tears. "We're coming out!" he called to the surface. "Grab the rope and pull."

Veronica and her dad pulled with all their might. Together, Maddy and the Captain swung out from the tunnel, dangling over the bottomless pit. Maddy screwed her eyes shut, only opening them again to the soft touch of Veronica's hands on her arms.

"Anything down there?" Veronica asked.

"Nope," said Maddy, "just an empty tube."

His head spinning, the Captain bit his tongue. "Girls, we can't stop for long," he said. "You have five minutes to gather as many diamonds as you can."

Maddy dumped diamonds by the handful into her pack, crowding poor Lucky Bunny. Veronica had no intention of settling for diamonds when she had come for pearls. She dangled her diamonds at the ends of strings and tied the strings to the straps on her pack, futzing with tape to make it all work—leaving plenty of room inside for pearls.

Veronica's dad tapped worriedly on the iPad. "Captain, look here. You see this? The pressure is building. The magma wants out. We can't stay long."

The Captain laughed. "Why? Because your little toy says so? I'll go home right now if you like. I found something more precious than diamonds—more precious than pearls—down there," he said, gesturing to the geyser pit.

Veronica looked doubtfully at him. "What could be more precious than pearls?" she asked.

"How about the answer to the great mystery?" the Captain said. "The whereabouts of the missing diamonds! I saw grooves carved into the tube floor, two parallel grooves spaced a foot apart. Someone wheeled a heavy cart through there, maybe thousands of carts.

"Don't you see? That's how the Diamond King smuggled out all the diamonds. He used the lava tubes like secret passageways, probably to bring the diamonds out to sea, to put them on ships. I bet you a trillion dollars' worth of diamonds they're out there still—somewhere, waiting to be found."

Veronica began to believe. She imagined a vast treasure scattered among shipwrecks just off the coast. "The treasure could be ours!" she said. "We just have to look."

"I told you already," her father said, *"there are no missing diamonds.* The very idea is preposterous—that a primitive people connected a vast network of tunnels under some of the most active volcanoes in the world. Then, a mysterious man, unknown to history, used those same tunnels to transport millions of tons of the most valuable gem on earth, which are now missing . . .

"I'm afraid it's not possible. A simpler explanation is more likely. The grooves you saw, Captain, could have been made by anyone or anything at any time. You don't need a Diamond King to explain a few scratches in a rock."

"Is that a fact?" the Captain snarled. "And what about the diamonds that just exploded all over your daughter? How do you explain those?"

"Easily enough," he said. "Diamonds are forged deep underground—right?—under enormous pressures. It's volcanoes that take them to the surface. All we are is lucky—at the right place at the right time—nothing more. It doesn't mean there are any *missing* diamonds. Besides, we're not here for diamonds. We're here to climb Mount Mystery. And the top is just ahead. It's time we did what we came here to do!"

The Captain disagreed with all of it, except for the last part, the old-fashioned bit. "Fine," he said in a low grumble, "we'll finish what we started, and then we'll go."

The girls collected diamonds while the Captain reattached the safety rope to their belt loops. "Be more careful this time," he said, fastening Veronica's dad. "I don't want to have to save you again."

Together, they continued up the volcano, but not as before. Now, the men hurried to keep pace with the girls. Somehow, despite many extra pounds of diamonds, the girls' steps felt lighter, the terrain easier, the climb less steep. Maddy and

Veronica rushed headlong toward the peak, chattering away, while the men followed in silence.

"Veronica?" Maddy said in a dreamy voice. "How many diamonds do you think we'll find up there? I bet the top is just one gigantic diamond."

Veronica nodded. "Yes, and the lava tubes—I bet they're full of diamonds too."

Maddy giggled. "We're going to be the richest girls in school."

"No," Veronica said. "We're going to be the richest girls in the world!"

A barrage of softball-sized lava bombs interrupted their daydream. A thick smoke rolled over them. Now they could see nothing—not even each other. They could only listen—to the low-pitched moans of lava fire and to the haunting sounds of an angry earth.

"Welcome to the caldera, girls," the Captain said, "the topmost crater. Stay to the outside. There's a magma lake in the center. We'll follow the ridge arou—"

As if on cue, Veronica slipped again in the loose sands. She collided with her father, and they tumbled like dominoes, knocking down Maddy next, and then the Captain, who this time could not stop their fall. Bound by rope, they slid together toward the seething cauldron of the volcanic core.

As he slid, the Captain pulled Maddy and Veronica on top of him. The girls rode him like a sled over the jagged rocks and hot stones. Veronica's dad slid next to them, in his now-familiar position—face first and on his belly.

The dense smoke glowed redder as they fell. "Girls!" the Captain cried. "We must stop! Drag your feet!" They dug into the earth with their boots and fingernails, clawing and scratching to save their lives. But they only gained speed, hurtling headlong toward their fate.

And then they glimpsed it—a vast red hole, a fiery grave, hissing with the honesty of death. They knew now they could not be saved. They screamed, the earth-fire raged, and they plummeted.

Thud! The rope pulled taut just in time, dangling the group over a red cauldron of instant death. The sweat poured off of them in sheets. Veronica felt the Captain's arms tighten around her. She squeezed Maddy, and Maddy squeezed back. "Thank God!" she breathed.

Then she glimpsed it—the broken figure of her father through the smoke. His arms and legs drooped askew around a blood-smeared boulder. His limp body anchored them to the earth.

"Daddy," she cried. "DADDY!"

The Captain clawed his way to Veronica's father. "Wake up! Can you hear me?" he yelled. But he did not wake up. The Captain felt for signs of life—a heartbeat, a pulse, a breath, anything.

Veronica sobbed into her father's breathless chest. The Captain searched himself for the words she would never understand—that her father was gone, that he had saved them all with his final act. But they had to go—and right now—or it would all have been in vain.

"Verr . . . onn . . . i . . . ca," came a soulful whisper. Her father's eyes blinked open. He saw the fuzzy outlines of his daughter's watery face. "I . . . love . . . you . . . more . . . than love," he said, his voice stronger with each word.

"But I love you more than that!" she sobbed.

"Can you hear me?!" The Captain said, leaning over him. "What's your name?! WHERE ARE WE?!"

"I'm Veronica's dad, this is Mount Mystery, and *please* stop yelling," he said, clearly but weakly. He staggered to his feet, the fog of concussion fading by the second.

The Captain cleaned the gash at his hairline, then checked him for other wounds. "You'll be okay," he said through a half-smile. "It was only superficial. Are you sure you were knocked out? Anyway . . . can you walk?"

Veronica's dad took a few halting steps, then nodded. "Let's get out of here."

Amidst the drama, Maddy opened her pack and checked on Lucky Bunny. The bunny peeked out, peered over the crater's edge, and let slip a tiny squeak of fright. A red sea of churning magma filled a hole in the earth a mile across and unknowably deep. Lucky's fur glowed red in the magma light.

Maddy was trying to console her, when she noticed something on the crater's edge. *No, it can't be*, she thought. She stooped down and scooped something from the hot ash with her bare hands. She bent down for a second handful, then a third. "Could it really be so simple?" she said.

Veronica's father frowned.

Veronica watched the pearls glow red against Maddy's

hands. Dirty, round, and ruby red, the volcano pearls clung to-gether like magnets, glowing as if illuminated by the lava itself.

Maddy counted them quickly in her hands. She had at least one hundred, more than enough for her own volcano pearl necklace. Veronica chose not to grab any, too concerned with the gash on her father's head to think of pearls. Besides, she wanted white ones.

"Enough pearls!" the Captain said. "We have to get out of here before we cook." But he was blinded by smoke, and judg-ing by their slide, they had a long, maybe impossible, hike back to the ridge.

Suddenly, a rainbow beamed out of the white-grey haze, as if a door had opened in front of them. The rainbow extended to the pearls in Maddy's hands. "The pearls are leading the way!" she said. Through the fog, they followed the rainbow up the crater wall, dodging mud pots and lava bombs, as if by magic, as if the rainbow or the red pearls or maybe the universe itself *wanted* to keep them alive, at least for now.

The smell of the sea told them they were close. A blast of salty air cleared the smoke, revealing a cloudless sky. Here was the ridgeline at last. Maddy stashed the red-glowing pearls into her pack, noticing they went instantly dull the moment they left her hand.

The adventurers looked out at Fire Bay, its waters as calm as a pane of blue-green glass. Across the bay, the skyscrapers of New Lava City glinted in the glare of the noontime sun. The hot black sands of the far side stretched for miles, speckled with pink and purple fireweed and gardens of cactus and wildflower.

There beside Fire Bay, beside the steaming crater, beside family and friends, they stood under a yellow sun. Veronica tried not to blink, burning the memory of the moment into her brain forever.

But she did blink. And when she opened her eyes, she noticed a large plume of pale green gas belch out of the earth near the coast. She noticed something else too, the faraway figures of an old man and a boy. They were searching for pearls in the black sands, the green gas heading straight for them.

Broken Boy

CHAPTER 19

Maddy and Veronica yelled, but the old man and the boy could not hear them. They were too far away and too busy, searching for pearls amidst the black sands, blissfully unaware of the gas cloud heading their way.

From atop Mount Mystery, the Captain peered through his binoculars. "It's them all right—the people from the bridge." He then pronounced their fate: "The gas will hit the boy but miss the old man."

"But we're going to save them, right?" Veronica said, not quite sure how. "I mean, we can't just let them die."

"Veronica," her father began, in his most understanding tone, "I wish we *could* do something. But it would take hours to get down there, and we can't risk it, not with the volcano this unstable. Besides, by the time we reached them, it would probably be too late. I'm afraid there's nothing we can do."

"Ugh . . ." the Captain grunted, "there is *something* we could

do. There's a lava sled in my pack." He retrieved a paper-thin foil rectangle and unfolded it to a surprisingly large size. A red plastic handle jutted out from its center. He pulled it, and the raft inflated instantly. "It's untearable and heatproof," he said, "and can get down to the bottom in under two minutes."

Veronica's dad rolled his eyes at the Captain's unexpected gadget. He answered his daughter's gaze. "I want to help them too," he said, his head still aching. "But I can't risk you again, Veronica. Think of your mother. What would she have me do? Risk your life to save a stranger's?"

Down the volcano, the old man and the boy finally noticed the pale green danger. The old man took off running, waving wildly at the boy and pointing at the cascading cloud. The boy heard him, looked up, and ran for the bay.

The Captain pressed the binoculars to his eyes. "He's heading for the water," he said. "But he won't make it."

Just as the boy's feet reached the water, the gas cloud enveloped him. He disappeared for a minute, obscured by the cloud. The gas dissipated, and they saw him again—floating in the blue waters of Fire Bay, lifeless and face down. The old man stumbled toward him, slowed by Mount Mystery's deep sands.

"Dad, we have to do something," Veronica said. "The volcano could explode in fifteen minutes, fifteen days, or fifteen years. But if we don't get down there—and I mean right now—they're both going to die."

He knew she was right; the old man was too weak to save the boy but would never leave him. *Yes, they would both die, but Veronica did not have to join them. Not everyone can be saved*, he wanted to tell her. *Sometimes, you have to save yourself.*

He looked her in the eye and saw the memories he would ruin: Babeltown, *Chowilawu*, the first view of Mount Mystery—they would all fade. But not this. This was the indelible moment, the life-changing event. And he climbed onto the sled.

Veronica hurried to the front. Maddy jumped on behind her. Lucky poked her head out of Maddy's pack and hopped into Veronica's lap.

"How does this thing steer?" Veronica asked.

"It doesn't," said the Captain, and he climbed onto the back, pushing off with both hands. The lava sled zoomed down the volcano, black sands kicking up along the sides. A mini-avalanche followed them down the slope.

Two minutes later, they reached the level base of Mount Mystery's far side, traveling at well over fifty miles per hour. Dragging their booties in the sands, they slowed themselves, skidding to a stop near the water's edge. The motionless boy lay just ahead of them, floating face down.

Slowed by the deep ash, the old man reached the boy at the same time. Together he and the Captain dragged him to land. The scent of pepper and pineapple hung in the air.

"Why? God? Why?" the old man cried.

The Captain, certified in CPR, remembered his training. He covered the boy's mouth with his own and puffed twice into his lungs. He began chest compressions, pumping the boy's chest thirty times in twenty seconds.

"We're here to help," Veronica's dad told the old man.

"HE'S DEAD!" the old man wailed. "MY GRANDSON! I KILLED HIM!"

"It's not your fault," Veronica's dad said. "And he's not dead. We can save him. But you have to believe."

The old man could see plain as day that the boy was not breathing. He fell to his knees. "MY DAUGHTER! MY BABY! I KILLED HER SON! TELL HER I'M SORRY. TELL HER I LOVE HER. AND TELL HER I STAYED!"

"But we're here to save you," Veronica's dad said.

"LEAVE US BE!" the old man bellowed. "I'm nothing without the boy. He wanted pearls—he wanted them so bad—he woke us at two in the morning. He made us hike at top speed—and for what? . . . So those girls wouldn't get here first and take them all. All this pain—all for pearls—all for nothing."

Veronica noticed the round impressions in the boy's pockets. She placed her hand on the old man's shoulder. "Did he find any black ones?" she asked.

The old man's watery eyes flashed red. "How dare you?" he spat. "How dare you ask me about pearls?"

But Veronica's dad understood. "Any hope that boy has is in his pockets," he said. "Stay out of our way." He positioned himself between the old man and the boy and winked at Veronica.

Veronica stooped over the boy's lifeless body and rummaged through his wet pockets, separating out all the black pearls and letting the others fall into the ash.

"Don't you touch him!" the old man shouted, lunging at her from his knees.

Veronica's dad stopped him. "She's not taking his pearls. She's trying to help. The boy has been poisoned. Can't you smell it? That's chlorine gas. He can't breathe."

The color drained from the boy's face, and his fingertips turned blue. Death closed in.

Veronica handed the pearls to her father. He pulled a full canteen from his pack and deposited them one by one inside. "I'm making Black Pearl Tea," he said to the old man. "Black pearls can stop some poisons. But it needs to be hot."

Veronica pointed at a nearby steam vent. "There!" she said. "Boil it over that."

Her dad sprinted to the vent and dangled the canteen over the steaming hole. The pearls hissed and rattled, popping like corn in the microwave.

The Captain continued his CPR, compressing the boy's chest over and over in rhythm, humming to himself the tune "Stayin' Alive" to time the beat. Maddy and Lucky Bunny watched from the lava sled, waiting for a miracle.

The minutes ticked by. The Captain felt the boy's lips go cold against his own. He could see the boy's still chest. Death had won. He stopped his CPR and stood up. "Your snake oil can't save him now," he called to Veronica's dad. "This boy is dead."

The old man crumpled to the ground, his body heaving. In the black sands on the far side of Mount Mystery, under a clear summer sky, the old man cried out to God: "You took the wrong one!"

Veronica's dad raced to the boy. He emptied the piping hot liquid down his throat. The boy convulsed as if his soul had fallen out of the sky and collided with his body. He vomited seawater into the black sands. Color returned to his face and warmth to his hands. His breath came shallow and uneven, but it came.

The old man clasped his hands to his face. "He's alive!" he sang. "Hallelujah! MY BOY'S A-L-I-I-I-V-V-E."

The boy opened his eyes. He could see only fuzzy outlines. The chlorine gas had burnt him. One eye was black, the other bloodshot and puffy. Half-blind and mute, he writhed on the ground in agony, the side of his head buried in the sand.

His grandpa tried to lift him, but the boy refused.

"Yes, don't get up," Veronica's dad said gently. "We'll carry you out. Keep your energy."

The boy shook his head. He shushed them with his index finger.

"He hears something," Veronica said. "It's in the ground."

The boy, who had not spoken in years, moved his mouth as if he expected a word to come out. Veronica put her ear to his lips. Then, it happened. The boy spoke.

He spoke a single word, but he spoke it clearly: "RUN!"

White Pearl

CHAPTER 20

"RUN!" The word—it started in the pit of his stomach, rolled up to the back of his throat, then emerged per-fected from his lips. The boy uttered it with his whole soul. "RUN!" There it was again, a determined croak—a hushed, throaty groan.

Veronica looked up the volcano, searching for any smoke, any lava, any motion at all. But she saw only tranquility, a ma-jestic mountain crowned by a deep blue sky. "I don't see any-thing wrong, do you?" she asked.

The Captain shook his head, then pressed his ear to the ground. "I don't hear anything either," he said. "David, you've been through a lot, and you're very brave. But it's time to go. Let us take you home, huh? Let us help you."

The Captain bent down to help, but the boy flailed against him. "RUN!" David rasped again. "RUN!"

"The boy hears everything," the old man said. "There's something in the ground."

Maddy stared across the glassy calm waters toward New Lava City, searching for something—for anything—wrong. Lucky Bunny pawed at her legs, begging to be picked up. Maddy obliged and placed her in the pack.

Something large jumped out of the water, then another and another, then more and more until the whole bay foamed and frothed. Sharks, hundreds of them, leapt out of the water. Something terrible was happening just beneath the surface.

The waters swelled without breaking, as if a balloon, half the size of the bay, inflated somewhere deep. The balloon exploded. A plume of grey ash and gas erupted. The waves came in all directions, cresting and crashing on the black sands.

The ground trembled.

The Captain stooped down to the boy. "I'm sorry," he said, looking him in the eye. "We should have believed you. Now get on." His tone brooked no disagreement. David climbed onto the sled, along with the old man. "RUN!" the Captain called to the others. "RUN!"

They trudged through the deep sands toward Yellow Lake, the men pulling the sled and the girls running in front. Veronica had not lost hope—not yet. *Maybe it'll just put on a show*, she told herself, *just like my volcano.*

A low-pitched roar bellowed from the caldera. Maddy covered her ears and stumbled to her knees. The Captain scooped her up, depositing her next to David on the sled. A plume of grey ash puffed high overhead.

"We're not going to make it, are we?" Maddy said to the boy. David reached for her hand, and she took it. The earth continued to cough and groan. Thousands of lava bombs streaked through the sky like a storm of meteorites, splashing and plunking into the waters of Fire Bay.

"Stop!" the Captain yelled. "Off the sled! Now!" He turned the sled over. The six of them huddled under the makeshift shelter, cowering, as lava bombs struck dozens of times a second.

When at last the bombardment stopped, Veronica emerged. "The beach!" she cried. "It's covered in pearls!"

Thousands of white volcano pearls littered the charcoal sands. Veronica bent down to pick one up, as her grandmother had so many years ago.

"They're cold!" she said. "How can they be cold?" She stuffed as many as she could into her pack, including a heart-shaped one and six round ones the size of grapefruits.

The earth rolled. A deafening boom split the air, and a blast of ash wind bit at their skin. Terrified, Veronica willed herself to look up. The entire summit, including the ridge where they had stood just minutes ago, exploded in a great column of lava. Red-orange rivers raged down the volcano's slopes. *There's no escape*, Veronica thought. *We're trapped between the lava and the sea.*

Veronica's dad looked out across the foaming waters, then gestured to the Captain.

The Captain understood. He retrieved his binoculars and scanned the white-capped waters. "Hmm ... there's something there," he said. "A dot, in the distance. Give me the flare!" He knew no self-respecting captain—no matter how daring—would ever risk his ship and crew to sail toward an erupting volcano. But he fired the flare all the same.

Dwarfed by the eruption, a small blue flame streaked through the sky. The chance some distant crew might notice a flare amidst a backdrop of thousands of lava bombs was remote, if not precisely zero. The flare hung for a few seconds, arced back to earth, then burned out pointlessly in the chop.

The Captain peered through his binoculars. "The dot—it's getting larger!" he said. "THEY'RE COMING! WE'RE SAVED!"

The old man raised his canteen as if holding a champagne glass. "To the kindness of strangers," he said, toasting. "Hallelujah! And praise be to God!" And he drank.

The Captain fell wordlessly to one knee, gasping as if he had been punched in the stomach. The dot grew larger until at last its billowing red sails burst into view. The ship's twin masts, its long sleek hull, and the distinct markings of dragons on the sails left no room for doubt.

"The *Dragon Prau*!" Maddy yelled. "Pirates!" She realized at once why they had turned. "They're not coming to save us, are they?"

"No, I reckon not," the Captain replied. "They're coming to eat us."

Molten rock rivers snaked down the volcano's flanks, hissing into the sea and spilling a purple haze over the land and water. "Lava or cannibals? Take your pick," the Captain muttered.

"It'll be okay," Veronica said. "You're Captain John. These are the People of Wood. Just tell them who you are."

"I told you already," the Captain said. "They're not the People of Wood—not anymore. They're scoundrels! Pirates! Cannibals! Besides, who can even speak their language?"

He watched the light of hope flicker and die in her eyes. "I'm sorry. You're right," he said. "There's always hope." But he didn't believe it. He emptied his pack. "Girls! Give me every last diamond you have. Fill my pack with diamonds."

Maddy opened her pack to the sight of Lucky Bunny looking up at her, not understanding. "You stay inside," Maddy told her. "No peeking. Don't come out, not for any reason." Maddy emptied her diamonds, while Lucky licked her hand, grateful for the extra room. Veronica, meanwhile, untied the strings of diamonds from her straps. Together, they filled the Captain's pack to the brim.

His hands shaking, Veronica's dad showed the Captain the iPad. "Where do you think they'll take us? Where should I send the lava car?"

A sticky, grey gob splattered the screen. A black rain began to fall. The Captain looked up at the ash column, now five miles high. "The ash fall has begun." He tapped the screen. "Here, send the car here—to Dream Cove. It's the closest bay, and there's a road nearby. We'll need them to take us there."

Veronica's dad set the location into the app, then looked back at the fast-approaching ship. He counted thirty pirates on the deck, some tending the sails, some watching the volcano, and others watching them. One, in particular, stood straight and strong, with a long bamboo blowgun pressed to his mouth.

"They can blow a poison dart in your neck from fifty yards," the Captain said. "Don't run! Lie on the ground!" The others listened. But the Captain remained standing, steadfast at the front of them all. He held the diamond pack high over his head.

"We can pay for safe passage!" he yelled. "We can pay for safe passage!"

The boat floated within ten feet of shore. A gang of men leapt out, shirtless, their bodies well-muscled and painted red. Each held a spear. Instead of pants, they wore plants—strips of bark tied immodestly to a string around their waists. Their grotesque earlobes hung down below their shoulders, stretched by heavy golden rings. They approached like a pack of black-haired wolves, patient and bloodthirsty.

A dog walked beside them. A golden retriever, it leapt off the boat along with the men, wagging its tail and darting playfully this way and that. Veronica hoped that a dog so happy and so fat was a sign that even man-eating pirates had a shred of humanity.

But then she saw their leader. He walked in the middle of the pack, one step ahead of the others. He wore a feathered headdress and a necklace of what could only be human teeth. Without breaking stride, he punched the Captain square in the jaw.

The Captain fell to the ground, his mouth filling with blood. "Don't struggle," he warned. "Don't struggle!"

A rush of syllables effused from the leader's mouth. His men understood each one. They grabbed the lava sled and all the packs and tossed them onto the ship. Lucky Bunny remained as still as possible—not peeking—not even once.

The pirates returned for their prisoners. One pirate bound their legs and another their arms. One by one, they dragged and tossed Veronica, her dad, Maddy, the Captain, the old man, and

David onto the boat like rolls of old carpet. Veronica landed face down on the hard deck, her nose scrunched against the urine-stained planks.

Escape!
CHAPTER 21

Thirty miles across the Bay, the people of New Lava City heard the explosions like cannon shots. They came out of their apartments and office buildings in droves, lining the water's edge, cell-phone cameras clicking.

Three hundred miles away in Crater Lake, Veronica's mom also heard the booms. She threw open the front door, certain to discover something terrible right outside—a car accident, a lava bomb, maybe even a meteor strike. But she saw nothing.

She checked her phone to see if anyone else had heard it too. She got her answer: everyone had. There in her feed, she watched the story unfold in real time: the towering ash column, the colorful lightning, the wild white water.

She gasped for air, drowning among the fearful posts and photos. She telephoned her husband, desperate to hear Veronica's voice, but she heard instead only the emotionless drone of the operator: "All circuits are busy now. Please try your call again later. Thank you."

Elyse knew something was wrong. "Mommy," she squeaked, "are Veronica and Daddy okay?"

"Yes, honey, of course they are," her mother said, her voice cracking. "They'll be home before you know it."

Veronica's mom checked the lava car app, expecting to find the car still parked at the entrance to the Cloud Forest. But she saw it was on the move. *Oh thank goodness*, she thought. *They made it!* She imagined her husband noticing the heightened volcanic activity and leaving immediately, before it got too bad. Then she saw the icon at the bottom of the screen: *Auto Drive*. And her heart sank again.

She dialed the phone dozens of times, until the impossible happened: It rang.

Veronica's dad felt his pants pocket buzz on the *Dragon Prau*. His arms and legs tied, he knew without looking who was calling. He saw his daughter, a prisoner of vile pirates on a vile ship, and he knew it was his fault. *It was reckless to continue past Magma Pass*, he thought. *It was reckless to cross Yellow Lake. It was reckless to go over the top. It was reckless to save the boy. And it would be his daughters and wife who paid for his mistakes.* He struggled against the ropes, but he was bound tight—helpless.

Mount Mystery smoldered under grey-black skies. The pirate leader commanded his men effortlessly, without speaking, his every movement a note in a symphony of seamanship. The sea pounded, the wind roared, and the pirate sailed—the diamond-filled backpack slung across his shoulder.

Thirty miles from shore the waters calmed. A pirate tended to a stove on the deck. He looked at Veronica and licked his lips. The fire roared to life. *Is this the flame we'll be cooked in?* she wondered.

His voice now shaky, the Captain continued to rasp, "We can pay for safe passage . . . we can pay for safe passage . . ."

"Enough!" Veronica's dad spat. "It's gibberish. Can't you see? They're savages. Save your strength."

For the first time, maybe in his life, the Captain knew defeat. "Girls, listen to me," he whispered. "The first chance you get, you jump overboard."

Veronica's tears puddled on the ironwood planks. She thrashed her bound arms and legs. "Let us go!" she raged. "Let us go! I want my mommy!"

The pirate leader stalked toward her. He grabbed her by the chin, forcing her eyes into his. He covered her screaming mouth with his hand. She could smell his rancid breath on her face and could taste his dirty hand on her tongue.

"Whare you fine dee diamons?" he demanded.

He reached for the knife on his hip. Its worn rhinoceros-horn handle told the story of the gleaming blade. Notches marked the number of lives it cut short, the souls it freed. He put the knife to her throat. "Tale me now—or I keel dee girl."

"I'll kill you! I swear it!" Veronica's father groaned. He convulsed on the deck, struggling against the ropes, his eyes glued to the knife.

"Yes, yes," the Captain said, negotiating. "We can take you there. Just don't hurt her. There's more diamonds, many more. We found them in a geyser. I can take you there. Let me show you."

The pirate gestured at the active eruption, the ash column now twenty miles high. He let go of Veronica's face. "You sin," he hissed, stalking toward the Captain. "YOU LIE! No take dare—not now. It gone."

"No, no!" the Captain said. "There's more, I promise!"

The pirate stooped down, staring the Captain in the face. "Who you be?" he demanded.

"I am Captain John—Captain John the 17th."

"YOU LIE!" said the pirate. And he stabbed him, slicing from his belly to his neck.

The Captain cringed, waiting for the gush of warm blood. But it never came. Only his shirt had been cut, sliced clean off. He felt the ash wind on his bare skin. The pirate kicked him onto his belly and beheld the ancient tattoo.

"My great . . . father tole of you," the pirate said. "I know you."

"Yes," the Captain said. "I am he—Captain John. Take the diamonds, and I'll bring you more. Just—please—let us go."

"*Pleez, pleez, pleez,*" the pirate taunted in a shrill high voice. He put his face in the Captain's. "I weel let *you* go. But price must be paid. Flesh must be paid. Pick one . . . save rest."

"Take me!" the Captain said. "And let them go!"

"NO!" the pirate thundered. "Pick one . . . save rest." He waved his hand over the prisoners. "Eat one . . . save rest."

The Captain spat in his face. "No," he said. "You disgrace your people. You disgrace God."

"God?" snarled the pirate. "Death my god! Eat one . . . save rest." And he thumbed at the strand of teeth around his neck.

The Captain closed his eyes. How badly he wanted to save his daughter. *Any name but hers,* he thought. *The boy and the old man would be dead already were it not for him. What harm in choosing the old man?* Stone-faced, he opened his eyes. "No," he said.

"All die!" growled the pirate. He dragged a finger across his throat, the universal sign of death. Six pirates came forward, with knives drawn.

The old man rolled to the leader's feet. "No!" he begged. "Choose me! Take me!" he cried, flashing a sad, toothy grin, as if offering his teeth as jewelry. "Take these!"

"I *weel*, ole man," the pirate said. "Now you die."

David squeaked.

"Turn away, boy," said the old man. "Tell your ma I'm sorry."

The pirate hoisted the old man to his feet. He pressed the gleaming blade to his neck, staring into his wide open eyes. "You brave, dead man," he said.

A bright light reflected off the gleaming blade. The old man's bones appeared as shadows through his living flesh. The pirate turned, just in time, to watch the earth swallow Mount Mystery whole.

An instant later, the magma chamber deep beneath Mount Mystery met the air, superheating it. The hot air rose and cold air rushed in. A whirlwind of flame exploded for miles in every direction, setting three of the ship's seven sails ablaze.

The shock wave knocked the leader backward into a mast. The dog tumbled across the deck into his arms. Half the crew blew overboard, swallowed by the sea. The other half clutched the ship's rail, holding on for dear life.

Thousands of fireballs, some the size of city blocks, streaked through the sky. The lightning came everywhere and at once, flashing so thick and so quick that it shone like noontime. Great elbowed spears of electricity pounded the waters all around them. The thunder boomed unbroken—continuous—as if there were no other sound in the world, only thunder.

Great tornadoes fell out of the sky like the fingers of God come to earth. Flocks of seabirds, their feathers ablaze, streaked through the sky like fireworks. The end of time had come.

The tips of the ship's masts erupted in an unburning flame of tripointed fire. The surviving pirates gaped at the blue-white torches—knees knocking, mouths open, eyes upcast—as if evil spirits had boarded the boat and affixed their ghostly lamps to its pointed masts. The pirates fled to the cabin below—all but one. The leader remained on deck.

"It's just St. Elmo's Fire," the Captain explained, his hairs standing on end. "It's the electricity in the air. It can't hurt you." The Captain turned to the leader. He saw a man ready to die. The wildness in his eyes was gone, replaced not with fear but with calm. "Cut us loose!" the Captain pleaded. "We'll be your crew!"

The pirate nodded. The ship was his birthright, his only possession. The sea would not have it—not without a fight. Against cyclonic winds, he pulled himself hand over hand along the ship's rail, toward his prisoners. With a flick of his blade, he sliced through their ropes. Veronica rose off the dirty planks and gazed at Mount Mystery.

But the mountain was gone. In its place a vast, glowing ash column heaved out of the sea. And then she saw it—a fire-tipped wave—a mountain of water, hundreds of feet high.

"Captain!" Veronica screamed: "Tssssuuuunnnnaaaam-mmmi!"

The Captain heard the wave like the hissing of a million snakes. His first thought was relief—if death had to come, at least it would be at sea. But death had other plans. "It's going the other way!" he cried. And then it dawned on him. "New Lava City!"

David's heart broke. "Maaaa!" he shrieked. The boy ran toward the ship's stern. He approached the railing without slowing, as if he planned to dive into the violent waters, swim to shore, and save his mother all by himself.

The old man tackled him to the deck. "It's okay," he said, "it's okay." But the boy knew better. His heart and soul emptied so he could not think or breathe. His cries hollowed to heaving sobs. Fatherless and brotherless, now motherless too, he screamed himself unconscious.

Across the bay in New Lava City, hell unfolded. The shock wave ripped through the streets, shattering every windowpane, turning the hot sulfurous wind into a murderous shrapnel cloud. Now the waters came. Skyscraper after skyscraper fell like Lego towers, and still the tsunami came, foaming and churning, raging inland—swallowing the city as if it were nothing at all.

Three hundred miles away, Veronica's mom followed every post. She saw the black sky, the scalding ash, and the tragic trampling on the bloody streets. Everything was panic, as if the madhouse had flung open its doors—people running in underwear and bare feet, men trampling children, and women begging the heavens for mercy. And then all at once, the flood of ghastly photos stopped. She tapped the refresh button. Then she tapped it again—still nothing, no more photos, no more status posts, no more sadness—just total, cataclysmic silence.

Dream Cove

CHAPTER 22

"Where we be?" the pirate called into the creeping darkness.

The needle of the Captain's compass spun like a toy top. "It's the ash," he said. "It's iron, and it's everywhere. Every speck is the North Pole to this thing." And he chucked the useless instrument into the foaming sea.

"I take sail. You take wheel," the pirate barked.

Meanwhile, Maddy and Veronica lay doubled over on the deck, clutching at their chests, unable to breathe. The wind, hot and choking, smelled of eggs and smoke. The pirate tore a dirty rag in half, tied it behind their heads, and covered their mouths. The rag filtered the ashy air. "Now you breathe," he growled. "Now you sail."

The ship's timbers screamed under the pressure of the pounding waves. Battered, they continued on, through gale-force gusts and swirling waters that would have capsized an ordinary crew. Mountainous waves hit the boat broadside, but the pirate and the Captain fought back, slipping into the dangerous troughs between waves, only to emerge and do it again.

Veronica did her part, helping on the sails, doing whatever the pirate barked. But the jolting, turbulent swaying made her seasick. She heaved her guts all over the deck and noticed the dog do the same. The deck stank of their retch, like an ocean of soured milk. She thought back to the last moment with her mother. She wanted another hug, and she wanted to go home, but right now she would have settled for less—for a wave to come, smash the boat, and end her misery.

Miles passed, the sea calmed, the lightning subsided, and the darkness came—total darkness. A darkness so extreme, it was not the opposite of light but the opposite of being. It was the Big Bang before the bang. It was the earth without form and void. It was darkness upon the face of the deep. Mount Mystery was gone, yet it was all around them—a blanket of blackness blotting out the sun. Trillions of flecks of pulverized rock hung in the air, filling their nostrils and lungs, deafening all sound. And still the crew sailed, as if with a third eye, into the raging dark.

Maddy smelled it first, then Veronica, then all of them. Gas flooded their lungs and bit at their skin. Veronica fell on her knees, first vomiting then dry-heaving. Maddy fell to the deck writhing, as if on fire. The pirate coughed so hard, it seemed his chest would split in two. Veronica's father choked on his own tongue, mumbling for his daughter. The old man crumbled to the ground, bleeding from his nose and mouth. The boy, already unconscious, groaned. Each of them collapsed in his or her own way—each of them except the Captain.

Captain John held his breath. He had saved more lives in water rescue than any diver in Crater Lake's history. He held the Crater Lake Volunteer Fire Department record, once holding his breath for more than seven minutes. He knew this feeling, and he knew it well. He was suffocating—drowning on his feet. Still, he sailed, until the last traces of oxygen dissipated in his blood, until his body convulsed and his chest seized. He slumped over, his hands on the spokes, asleep at the wheel.

The boat listed in the wind.

Time passed. Veronica's eyes blinked open to Lucky Bunny licking her face. She looked up into the heavens. Cloths of violet velvet settled on the horizon. The sun sank like a stone through the purple haze.

She sat up slowly, her head aching and her skin covered with sores. Heaps of ash covered the boat's every surface. She felt her father's limp hand on hers. She watched him beside her—his chest rising and falling, his eyes shut, not moving. She let go of his hand, lifted herself up, and peeked over the railing, as if into a painting.

A painted sea lapped a painted cove under a painted sky. Hundreds of small rock islands jutted out of the cobalt water like towers, crowned in green, and circled by thick tangles of mangroves. She spun around and fell to her knees. "LAND!" she called.

A green jungle ringed a white-sand beach. The boat, adrift in the warm breeze, skidded across the sands, coming to rest in a place that could only be Dream Cove.

Veronica saw the Captain. He hung by his armpits from the ship's large wheel, passed out on his feet, his shirt smoldering on the ground beside him. She studied the tattoo on his bare back. Something about it was familiar.

Her heart raced. Tears welled in her eyes. *It couldn't be*, she thought. *How could he not know?* She needed the iPad, the one in her father's backpack, and she needed it now.

She found her pack first, lying ten feet away in deep ash, soaked by waves. The lumpy outlines of large pearls bulged out of the bottom.

She poked her hand into another mound, then another and another, uncovering in turn Maddy, David, the old man, and even the dog—all unconscious but breathing. She cleared the ash from around their mouths and continued to search. She eyed another mound, reached in, and pulled it out—her father's pack.

She pointed the iPad camera at the Captain's back and zoomed in. She snapped photo after photo, carefully capturing the web of crisscrossing lines and the two triangles at the top left and right corners.

She had seen this pattern before—many times—near her own house. She thought they were lava tubes. Her whole family thought they were lava tubes. But what if they were wrong?

Her father stirred. She slipped the iPad back into his pack and returned it to the ash.

Her father's eyes blinked open. "VERONICA!" he gasped.

"Hey, Dad," she said, waving. "It's okay. We made it. Look!"

Through blurry eyes, he considered the paradise around him. *It's heaven*, he thought, disappointed. He wished Veronica

were not there, not yet. He thought of his broken-hearted wife and knew that he had failed.

Veronica saw his dreaming eyes. "Dad, it's okay! We made it!" she repeated. He plodded toward her on unsteady legs. He stumbled, landing on something big and warm, just beneath the surface. He dug into the ash.

The serene face of the pirate leader greeted him—eyes shut, bloodied but alive. Veronica's dad smiled. He straddled the pirate's chest and knotted his fist.

"DAD!" Veronica yelled. "NO!!"

His eyes unglazed, and his fist unclenched. She could see now that he was himself. "What about the others?" he rasped. Veronica turned white. She had forgotten the pirates down below.

"Well, we can't just leave him here," her father said. "We need rope."

Veronica returned to the place where her own hands were freed. She reached into the ash, pulled out a length of rope, and handed it to her father. As she did, she saw for herself the pirate leader sprawled out on the deck, his unconscious hands still clutching the diamond pack. She ripped it from him, then slung it over her own shoulder, where it belonged.

Veronica's dad kicked the pirate onto his belly. He tied his wrists, remembering the man's filthy hands on his daughter's mouth. He tightened the knot, then he tightened it some more, then he tightened it most viciously. With his foot on the pirate's back, he yanked up on the ropes, until they bled with his revenge.

He then unsheathed the pirate's knife and approached the

cabin door. The door creaked open, and he glimpsed the carnage inside. The purple face of the first pirate told the terrible tale. His tongue—swollen five times too big—oozed out of his dead mouth. Every man in the room met the same end: death by suffocation—on his own tongue.

"Are they in there?" Veronica asked, as her father returned to the deck.

"They won't be bothering us anymore," he said simply. He scanned the deck. "Hey Veronica, have you seen my pack? I need the iPad to find the car."

Veronica pretended not to know. "Maybe that's it?" she said, and she pointed to exactly the right ash mound.

He retrieved the iPad from the pack and checked the lava car app. "The car's right there," he marveled, "just beyond those trees." Eyes wide, he looked at the Captain, who began to groan. Soon, they all began to stir—Maddy, the old man, David, and even the dog.

The Captain grunted, lifted himself off the wheel, and rose to standing on wobbly legs. He realized where he was, took one look at Maddy, and could hardly believe his luck. "Well," he said, slapping Veronica's dad on the back, "I'm never going to Mount Mystery with you people again."

He noticed the diamond pack slung across Veronica's shoulder. "That bag belongs to him," he said, gesturing to the pirate. "I told him we'd pay for safe passage and here we are."

Veronica's mouth fell open. "What? But—he—he," she stuttered, "wanted to kill us . . . *and eat us!*"

"Actually, he only wanted to eat one of us," the Captain

deadpanned. "But here we are, safe and sound, in Dream Cove on his ship. And a promise is a promise."

Veronica's hazel eyes pleaded. "But Dad," she said, "those diamonds are ours!"

Veronica's dad wanted the diamonds too. "I know, sweetie," he said. "But it's the Captain's call. He's the one who promised the diamonds. And he's the reason we're still alive at all."

Her dream of diamond riches dashed, Veronica handed the Captain the pack. "Here you go then," she sighed. Her sad eyes fell on Lucky Bunny. She scooped her up and planted a kiss on her whiskered mouth.

The Captain lifted the pirate to his feet, plopping him down onto the ship's only chair. He slapped him in the face, doused him with water, yelled in his ear, but still could not rouse him. "He's out cold," the Captain said. He turned the sack of diamonds upside down and emptied every last one into the pirate's lap.

The Captain frowned at the bloody ropes. "We can't leave him tied like this," he said. "The birds would get him. He'd be dead by morning."

"I can live with that," Veronica's dad said.

"Well, I can't," said the Captain. "You cut that monster loose. I'll get the others to shore."

Veronica's dad grunted, without agreeing.

The Captain slung a rope ladder over the railing into the shallow waters. One by one, he ushered each person down the ladder and off the boat. "Veronica, you first . . . good. Now you, Maddy . . . good. David, you're next . . . David?"

But David did not move. Everything curious and passionate, mysterious and magical was gone. His blind eye peered into the blackness, and his other focused on the wave. He imagined his mother's final thought. *She died thinking he was dead.* And his heart broke again.

The old man tried to console him. He told him that life goes on, that things still matter, that no feeling is forever, that this grief too will pass. But still David did not move.

The old man climbed down the ladder. "Hand him to me," he said. "I'll carry him to the car." The Captain dangled David to the old man, then climbed down the ladder himself. Together, they carried the boy away from the ship and into the trees.

Veronica's dad scanned the ship a final time. He noticed the bamboo blowgun poking out of the ash. He picked it up, smashed it over his knee, and tossed both ends into the sea.

The pirate coughed and opened his eyes. Veronica's dad stalked toward him, knife in hand. "You deserve so much more than this," he said. He pressed the blade to his neck and flicked his wrist, slicing off the pirate's toothy necklace. "This is mine now," he said. "And one more thing . . . Captain John keeps his word." With a final flick of his blade, he freed the pirate's hands.

The pirate stared blankly ahead. One hand pawed at the diamonds in his lap, the other hung at his side. Something warm and wet slid across his limp hand; it was his dog's tongue. The dog barked, ready to play.

Veronica's dad clambered down the ladder. Just a hundred feet ahead, a dirt road no wider than a car cut through the trees. There was the lava car, parked and waiting. A red bird of paradise, its long tail feathers spread out like a fan, perched on the roof, chirping cheerfully.

The six of them crammed into a car made for five. In the backseat, David sat catatonic on the old man's lap, while Maddy sat in the middle holding Lucky Bunny.

"Dad?" Veronica asked. "Should we call Mom?"

"I wish we could," he said. "But there's no service. Try a text on the iPad. Maybe it'll go through."

Veronica opened the trunk. She removed the iPad from her father's pack for the second time that hour. She typed out a text: *Low batt. See u @ midnight. I <3 you.* The progress indicator read *Sending* . . . , but it never sent. This time, she slid the iPad into her own pack, not her father's, closed the trunk, and climbed into the backseat.

Lucky Bunny hopped into her lap, closed her eyes, and settled in for the long ride home.

Home Sweet Home

CHAPTER 23

No sooner had they started down the rutted road, than Veronica and Maddy fell fast asleep. David stared off into space, motionless, his face blank. The three men barely spoke.

None of them had driven to Dream Cove before. The road traveled far to the northwest, tracing interconnected valleys and weaving in and out of mountain ranges.

Fog settled upon the valley floor as the sun set. Through the windshield Veronica's dad saw nothing except the vague haze of a low moon and the white mist of reflected high-beam light. He set the car to autopilot. They passed not a single town or village—not even another car. The only light in the darkness was their own.

Six hours later the midnight lights of Crater Lake blinked into view. The Captain breathed a heavy sigh. He turned to the old man. "You and the boy are welcome to stay with me," he said. "We have plenty of room. You need a good night's rest. In the morning, we'll get the boy to a doctor and check in on the rescue."

The old man said nothing. He looked into space, his eyes as sad as the boy's.

"There's still hope for your daughter," the Captain said. "The wave—it was bad, but you don't know. And until you do, you have to believe, if not for you, then for the boy."

The car rolled to a stop in front of the Captain's house. The girls awoke, rubbing their eyes. Veronica's dad popped open the trunk. The Captain exited first, followed by Maddy and the old man. The old man carried the boy, and the Captain grabbed their packs, staggering to the door.

"Hey, Dad," said Veronica, groggily. "Leave the trunk open. I need something."

She slid out of the car, grabbed her pack, and returned to the backseat. "I don't want Mom to see Lucky until morning," she said, and she placed the still-sleeping bunny into her pack.

The lava car pulled away from the curb and headed for home. Veronica slipped off to sleep, waking again only as the car turned into her driveway. Warm yellow light streamed from every window, and every outdoor light was left on. Above her home, the volcano towered, shimmering in the light of a violet moon.

Veronica knew her mother was inside, awake and waiting. But as the garage door opened, she shut her eyes, pretending to sleep.

Her dad nudged her gently. "Veronica . . . Veronica . . . are you awake? Veronica?" But she did not move. He kissed her once on the cheek and unbuckled her seatbelt. At the sound of the garage, her mother rushed to them, but she hushed herself on seeing Veronica.

Veronica's dad winked at his wife. He picked up his daughter, her long legs dangling down nearly to the ground. He carried her out of the garage, up the stairs, and into her room, where he laid her down gently in bed. Her mother followed behind them, carrying Veronica's backpack.

"Let her sleep," her dad whispered. "She's been through a lot." He kissed her cheek and left the room.

Veronica's mom bent over her sleeping daughter, who was now cracking a smile. "I know you're faking," she said. "You just love carries and cuddles—like your dad." And with that, she planted kisses all over her face and tickled her ribs, until they were both rolling on the bed, howling with laughter.

Thud.

Startled, her mother stood up. "Did you hear that?"

Thud.

"There it is again . . . It sounds like it's coming from . . . *Eeekk!*" she screamed.

The backpack fell over, and Lucky Bunny spilled out, zigging and zagging in every direction.

The bunny hopped nervously this way and that. "Lucky! Over here!" Veronica yelled. The bunny ran at top speed toward the bed, leaping in a single bound over Veronica's mom's head and landing squarely on Veronica's chest.

"Can we keep her, Mom?" Veronica begged. "Please!"

"Keep her?" her mother scolded. "She *nearly* landed on my head!"

"But Mom, you won't even notice her, I promise," Veronica said, her hazel eyes pleading. "I'll feed her and clean her! Please, Mom! She saved my life!"

Veronica's mother smiled. "Only if you tell me how you two met," she said.

Veronica erupted. "The bunny saved our lives. We would have all been crushed, but she made us run away, but before that we made ash angels, and I saw our old house and my old room, and then we went to the grave and . . ."

Veronica went on and on, retelling the tale, from the cave and Magma Pass to the Cloud Forest and the shimmering diamonds of Mount Mystery.

Her story darkened with the pirate and the tsunami, then brightened again in Dream Cove. Veronica told of the purple sky and blue waters, and how the Captain had passed out at the wheel. But she left out an important detail—the secret of the Captain's tattoo.

"I just can't believe it!" her mother said. "I just can't believe it!" She repeated over and over, nodding and hugging and dabbing her eyes. "All in one day? I just can't believe—" Her voiced cracked, and the tears came, and she wept for the drowned souls of New Lava City.

"Mom, I brought you something," Veronica said consolingly. "Volcano pearls!"

"Show me!"

"Maybe on your birthday!"

"But they're *mmmaaaggggiiicccaaalll*," her mother said in a singsong voice. "If you show me . . . I'll prove it."

Veronica was almost certain there was no such thing as magic but not certain enough not to see whatever her mother had to show. "Fine," she said, "I'll show you, but just one and only a small one. She climbed out of bed and reached into her pack. She reached past the iPad and the six grapefruit-sized pearls. "Here you go!" she said, as she returned to bed.

Her mother admired the rare pearl. "You sure you don't want it—you know—for yourself?"

"Yes, Mom, I'm sure. It's yours."

Veronica's mom placed one hand on her daughter's cheek, while holding the pearl in the fist of her other. "May you always find what you seek," she said.

No sooner did she say the words than the house lights dimmed and the pearl flashed bright white. "Ouch!" she exclaimed. She opened her fist. The pearl in her hand had dematerialized in a wisp of white smoke. Where it should have been, there was nothing—only an imprint—a red, round, stinging burn.

Veronica ran her fingertips across her mother's palm. "Where did it go?" she asked.

"There's something you should know about your pearls," her mother said, laying her hand over Veronica's necklace. "Some say they're magic, even the source of all magic. I say they're a link—to a world we'll never understand, but we know is right. Your dad, he would laugh. He would say, 'It's all just science. There's no such thing as magic. What today we don't understand will tomorrow be understood.' And maybe he's right. But if it's science, it's the science of beginnings and whys—of what came before, of why we are here."

"Mom—" said Veronica in a small voice. "Do white pearls make wishes come true?"

"No," her mother laughed. "Of course not, Veronica. They're not genie lamps."

"Then what *do* they do?"

"That I cannot tell you," she said, "because I do not know. But I can tell you this: We know black pearls vanish in hot water. We know red pearls glow on human skin. And we know white pearls . . . we know white pearls are activated by dreams, by imaginings. Wishes upon them may never come true. But for the right dream, for the right imagination, maybe the universe will stop long enough to listen."

Veronica clutched her pearls silently.

"But if I were you," her mother continued, "I wouldn't mention any of this to your father. You see, your grandma taught me a thing or two about pearls. She wore them her whole life. She understood them as well as anyone. Their powers are strongest in the hands of a girl. But the pearls are never showy. They reveal themselves only to those who believe . . .

"But enough of all that," she said. "Look at my poor baby, all covered in scrapes and burns. It's time to put some lotion on you and get you to bed."

Veronica blinked a tear out of her eye. "But Mom—" she said, "I need to know. What about heart-shaped pearls?"

"A Heart?!" her mother gasped. "Why, a Heart is the most

special of all. I even had one once. Grandpa gave it to me. He told me heart-shaped pearls were activated by love—"

Her voice cracked. "Now, I don't know about all that. But I know this: Losing one breaks your heart. I brought mine with me on the *Minnehaha*. It slipped out of my hand. I watched it sink into the deepest waters of Crater Lake. I was careless. I was ten. But never mind . . . Why? Did you find one?"

"Umm . . . no," Veronica fibbed. "I thought I saw one, but I couldn't reach it."

"No bother," her mother said. "You're back and that's all that matters. You need your rest. Your sister's going to want to see you in the morning—bright and early. Now, get to sleep." She tucked her in, kissed her forehead, and pretended to walk away.

"Mom! You're forgetting something. The sauce!"

Her mother smiled. She held one hand to her lips and the other to her heart. Then she kissed her fingers and ran both hands gently down Veronica's face, brushing her eyelids, and continuing down past her belly button to the tips of her toes, making kissy noises all the while. "Here's your sleepy sauce, and here's your good dream sauce—it's about seeing your sister tomorrow."

"Lucky needs sauce too, Mom!" Veronica said.

"Bunnies don't get sauce," her mother harrumphed.

"Please, Mom!"

Her mother relented, spreading sauce on the bunny as well. "Now get to sleep," she ordered, "both of you." At the doorway, she switched off the lights and looked back at her daughter. "I love you more than love," she said.

"But I love you more than that," Veronica answered. She watched her mother slip out of the room, close the door, then open it again—slightly—leaving it just the right distance ajar.

In the hallway, her mother sobbed silently. She was relieved to have her daughter back safe and sound, but heartbroken for the people of New Lava City, for all the children who would never go home again. She cried until she had no more tears left to cry. She heard her husband downstairs and followed the noises into the kitchen.

"My jewelry box!" she said, sniffing. Her husband had just placed the dusty, wooden box on the kitchen counter. She rummaged through the tiny drawers, trying on rings and necklaces she hadn't worn in years. "I barely remember this stuff," she said. "I never thought I'd see it again."

He returned to unloading the car, then came back holding both hands behind his back. "Pick a hand," he said.

His wife smiled. "The left!"

He thrust forward his left. Her eyes lit up. "Oh my goodness! Veronica's blanket! The one Mom made!"

Then he showed his right.

"Your poem!" she gasped. "And look at those old photos. I can't believe it—I would have thought they all would have burned. What's Babeltown like?"

"Grey. But beautiful," he said, "like you . . . in thirty years."

She giggled, as he remembered, and he kissed her.

"I'm going to hang this now," he said, still holding the poem. "It's been too long."

"Just don't wake her," she said.

He tiptoed up the stairs, although he knew Veronica would still be awake. Inside her room, he scanned the walls for the perfect spot, deciding it best not to disturb her other hangings, especially the one of her favorite boy wizard.

He chose a bare wall next to the window. By the light of his cell phone flashlight, he tapped in a nail and hung the poem that he had written for her, so many years ago.

He turned to leave.

"Daddy," she said, without sitting up. "Can you read it to me?"

He kissed her forehead, held her hand, and sang her to sleep:

Bedtime for Veronica

As you lay in your crib
Holding my hand,
I think of your future
And the things I have planned.
Of skinned knees and bicycles
And trips to the zoo,
Of lollipops and fevers
And Mount Mystery too.
I laugh at the smile
that lights up my life,
And thank God for your mommy
Who I call my wife.

As the lullabies play
And the seahorse goes round,
You inspire my dreams
With each babbled sound.
I dream you're a teen
Dressing for prom,
I dream you're a woman
Just like your mom.
I imagine you glow
On your wedding day.
I imagine I'm the daddy
Who gives you away.

As you toss and you turn
Then finally lay still,
And your eyes start to shut
As they most certainly will.
I tell you a story
Of a sun that goes down
A moon that rises up
While the world spins around.
And you clutch your baby
And you hold her tight,
And you help her fall asleep
For a long, dark night.

As you let go of my hand
I don't hear a peep,

I count to sixty once
Just to make sure you're asleep.
For now, you're my baby
And I hope it goes slow,
I find so much joy
In watching you grow.
As I shut the door behind me,
Precious Veronica Pearl
I think to myself,
What a beautiful girl.

Gathering Gloom

CHAPTER 24

Veronica awoke shivering under the covers, squinting in the dawn light smeared across her bedroom window. Outside, brick-red snow fell in large clumps on the volcano. Ice-white crystals framed the windowpane like a painting—surreal and improbable.

She searched her closet for her fuzzy bunny slippers and warmest robe, then scampered down the stairs.

She found her father fiddling with the large stone fireplace in the living room. "Don't worry, I'll get the heat on soon," he said. "Didn't expect snow in the summer, eh?"

"But why's it red?" Veronica asked. "And why's it so cold?"

"It's Mount Mystery, sweetheart," he said. "The ash high in the atmosphere messes with the weather, scattering the sun's rays and cooling the air. The snow mixes with the ash. But it's a good thing. The ash clings to the snow and falls in clumps. With any luck, enough ash will fall to let the sun warm things up again. It's nature's way of cleaning itself off."

In the kitchen, Veronica heard the pitter-patter of little feet, then saw the golden-haired blur heading straight for her. "Elyse!" she called.

Elyse kept running. She collided with Veronica at top speed, hugging her so tightly that Elyse's little feet lifted off the floor.

Veronica squeezed back just as hard. She sniffed the sweet aroma of hot cocoa. "Making hot chocolate Elyse?" she asked.

Elyse gasped, as if she had forgotten. "Oh no!" Her eyes darted to the counter.

Veronica saw why. "The cup!" she yelled. But it was too late. The hot cocoa maker dispensed its contents all over the floor.

Veronica ran for the paper towels, dispensing about half a roll. On her hands and knees, she cleaned up her sister's mess, then prepared another cup of cocoa.

"Can I have two marshmallows this time?" Elyse asked. "One for the cup and one for my mouth?"

Veronica chose two marshmallows from the bag on the high pantry shelf. She completed Elyse's perfect morning drink with a huge pour of milk and a bendable straw.

"Do you want to play somethin'?" Elyse asked. "How 'bout sword fight?"

"I'll get the paper!" Veronica said.

At the kitchen table, between sips of hot cocoa and orange juice, the two sisters crafted paper swords, a paper shield, paper helmets, and even paper sword holders. They taped the sword holders to their waists and ran around the house doing battle, and mostly attacking their dad.

The family enjoyed their quiet morning at home, until a loud rumble rattled the windowpanes.

Veronica's dad looked outside. "Hmmm," he said, "that's not the volcano. It's thunder, or I guess you could call it *thundersnow*. It's just the weather—nothing to worry about."

Veronica shrugged. She ran for the playroom with her sister.

"Nothing to worry about?" his wife said in a concerned whisper. "You do realize when we last heard thundersnow, don't you?"

He smiled understandingly. "No, no," he said. "It'll pass. It's just the weather. This time it's different."

The phone rang, and Veronica's dad answered it. "Uh . . . hello?"

"*Hallo?* . . . some weather we're having!" boomed the Captain. "How's Veronica? Good? Good! . . . Listen, I just got word—survivors of New Lava City are streaming into town. There's a meeting at the church in an hour. But I'll be late. David's eye needs checking. It looks even worse today."

"Survivors?" Veronica's dad said, surprised anyone survived at all. "I guess I'll see you there. How's the rescue?"

"No rescue," said the Captain. "We don't know enough. We need to hear from the survivors. Anyway . . . I've got to go. I'll see you at the church."

Veronica's dad hung up the phone.

"Rescue?!" his wife demanded, in a tone somewhere between an argument and a question. "You are *not* going back to Mount Mystery. Promise me you won't. *Promise me!*"

He considered reminding her that Mount Mystery was

gone, exploded into a trillion flecks of ash, and that no one would ever go back there again. But he thought better of it. "I promise, sweetheart," he said. "That was John. He called to say that the first survivors have made it to town. There's a meeting at the church. I have to go, in case we can help—you know, with food and supplies."

Veronica and Elyse screeched into the room on their green and red scooters. Elyse carried a large pirate ship in one hand while steering with the other. "Dad, Veronica won't play pirates," she said. "And I really, *really* want to play pirates."

He tried not to laugh. "Umm . . . okay . . . well . . . Veronica may have had enough pirates for a while," he said. "And—you two—*please* play nicely. I have to run to town, but I'll be back in a bit."

Disappointed, Elyse flung herself onto the carpet.

"Run to town?" Veronica said. "What for?"

"Survivors from New Lava City," he said. "They've come to town."

"Then I'm coming too," Veronica said. "Please, Mom! Those poor people!"

Her mother frowned. As much as she had missed her, she did not care to spend the next hour or two entertaining a moping daughter. "Just get back in time for supper," she said.

The red snow fell in large flakes as the lava car rolled into town. Veronica looked out the window at the white church glowing red under a strange sky. She knew the building well, mostly from the outside. Many times her family had boated on the lake in bad weather, blinded by the fog and rain but beckoned to the town's docks by the bright light atop the church's bell tower.

Crowds thronged the building, making parking impossible. Veronica's father stopped the car in the middle of the street, just outside the church, and they stepped out together to a chorus of beeping horns. The driver of the car behind them gestured profanely. Veronica's dad checked that Veronica wasn't looking, then returned the gesture. He tapped his phone, and the lava car rolled away to go park itself.

Inside the windowless church, a foul smell permeated the building. On one side, hundreds of people—all strangers to Veronica—filled the pews, sitting silently in torn and tattered clothes, their faces blank and haunted. A silver-haired man, dressed all in white, gleamed amidst the dirty horde and tended to their many wounds.

Dozens more half-naked survivors lined the corridors at the front and back, as scores of townspeople squeezed into every remaining seat. A young girl in the front row stood waving excitedly at them. It was Makenna, Maddy's next-door neighbor.

Maddy and Makenna lived next to each other on Crater Lake. Along with Veronica, who came to visit whenever she could, the three girls spent many summer days hanging out on the docks—fishing for sunnies, jumping in the lake, and boating over to Diamond Island for a bit of diamond hunting.

At the front of the church, next to Makenna, sat a man in a blue policeman's uniform. It was her father, Officer Steve, one of only three policemen in the whole of Crater Lake. A compact but powerful-looking man, he was as friendly as he was strong.

He'd personally built the wooden ramp that connected Maddy's dock to Makenna's, creating one giant, lakefront playground.

"We saved you a seat," Officer Steve said. "The big man said you'd be coming."

Veronica and her father slid into the aisle. Veronica whispered excitedly, "We were there, Makenna! At Mount Mystery! We found diamonds! And there's more!"

Makenna rolled her eyes. "Oh please!" she tutted. "You always know where the treasure is, don't you? How many holes have we dug on Diamond Island? And how many diamonds have we found?" She made a zero with her hand.

Veronica stuck out her tongue and dug into her pocket. She produced a loose, white volcano pearl. "Well, sometimes I'm right," she said. "And we did find diamonds, really, we did—a whole bag full."

"Then show me," Makenna said.

Bang. Bang. Bang.

At the front of the congregation, the mayor of Crater Lake, Sal Besboff, banged his heavy hand on the podium. He had a thick neck, a bald head, and a bushy grey mustache. His belly swelled as if he had swallowed a bowling ball. He wore a tight-fitting suit jacket that looked as if it had not been buttoned for a decade. His tie stretched down no further than his navel.

"The meeting will come to order, the meeting will come to order," Besboff barked with no effect. His voice carried no more than a few rows into the chattering masses, and even those people paid him no attention.

The din of neighborly conversations grew louder, and all

from one side of the chamber. "Strange weather we're having, isn't it?—Red snow? Never in all my years—Look at them, the poor dears, can you believe it?—Did you see the pictures?—No, it can't happen here, thank god!—Where should we send our canned goods?—It looks like they need clothes—And that smell, my goodness!—We should probably send soap!"

Scrreeeeeech!

The PA system squealed as the mayor fumbled with the microphone. "The meeting will come to order," he said again and again, his face redder each time. "The meeting will come to order." Finally, a great deal of shushing quieted the noisy chamber.

"We came here in the interests of humanity," the mayor began, significantly. "Our city friends need us. And if there's one thing I know about this town, it's that we always help our friends." He paused for effect, then turned toward the rows of survivors. "Please—would one of you join me at the podium? Please—tell us what you saw. Tell us how we can help."

A blonde woman, no older than forty, rose from her seat and hobbled to the podium. Her shredded dress revealed black burns on her alabaster thighs. Dirt stained her face, and patches of skull peeked out from behind her mud-matted hair. She wrapped her bony fingers around the microphone. "I have come from hell," she said:

> I saw the sea drain like a bathtub, with its plug pulled
> out. I saw the waters recede a hundred yards, then
> two hundred, then a mile. I saw whales and sharks

exposed on the seabed, flipping and flopping like goldfish in an empty bowl. I heard every train whistle blow, every church bell toll, every fire alarm blare—all at once, all in warning. I saw a dark mist. I saw many run. I saw others stop and stare. I saw people huddled on rooftops. I watched the buildings fall.

The woman's mind raced behind her eyes. The microphone shook in her hand. She could see it all so clearly, as if the wave were striking again right there in that church. Her frantic eyes fell on the man in white. He smiled at her, and she continued:

I saw children sheltering stuffed animals. I saw whole families crushed and swept away. I saw dead hands grasping for the surface. I saw wide-open mouths, struck dead midscream. I saw rafts of corpses bobbing on a blood-red tide. I saw the end of the world. I saw the judgment day.

Her voice cracked. Her tears fell upon the podium. The mayor, now ashen-faced, patted her on the shoulder. "Please—take your time. How did you get here? How many survived?"

She looked again to the man in white and swallowed hard. She continued:

We walked and we walked—through flooded towns and obliterated villages, villages of the dead: old men, young girls, men in suits, women in rags, all dead. We saw the shadows of death—the last moment—children running, priests praying—all reduced to dust, to black outlines on brick walls, to incinerated imprints of stolen life.

And still we walked. We walked for miles—no voices, no cries, no sounds . . . and then I heard it . . . a child writhing and whimpering: "Water! Water!"

The child, her face it was charred, her body black, her lips no longer lips. I poured the last of my water into her open mouth. She sputtered it into the ash. She couldn't swallow.

She had swallowed the fire.

And so we walked, bare feet bleeding, unsure if the volcano had consumed the whole world. Finally, we crossed the death line. We found cars that could run and roads that could be passed, and we came here . . .

"Did you pass by South Lavafield?" cried a man.

"How about Cratertown?" sobbed an old woman. "My daughter's in Cratertown."

"What about Los Asheles?" called another.

The woman at the podium cleared her throat: "Those towns are gone. Those people no longer exist. What has begun, I'm afraid . . . is only the beginning. This town is *next*."

The room gasped. "What do you mean . . . *n-n-next*?" the mayor stammered.

The church door creaked open. Sunlight spilled into the dimly lit chamber. Every soul on the left side turned, expecting the angel of death to burst forth and smite them where they sat. Instead, the Captain bounded in, trailed by Maddy, David, and the old man.

"David!" breathed the woman at the podium.

The boy's one good eye focused on her. He let go his grandfather's hand. "Maaaa!" he cried, sprinting toward her.

The never-forgotten sound of her son's own voice washed over her. "I thought I lost you," she sobbed.

He leapt into her arms. The mother and son hugged in an embrace that held the whole world and could have lasted just as long.

At last, she looked at the old man, her father. He reached for her as if she were a ghost, as if his hand would pass right through her. "How?!" he sobbed. "How?!"

The woman pressed her finger to his mouth. Her gaze turned to the man in white, his clothes clean and unburnt, his fiery blue eyes unblinking in the bright church spotlight.

"Him!" she said, pointing. "*He* saved us."

Something to Say

CHAPTER 25

The man in white smiled at the woman and rose from his chair. He glided toward the podium, his wild silver tresses cascading down his shoulders. "I told you he would come, didn't I?" he whispered, brushing his hand against her tear-streaked cheek. "Have faith, my child . . ."

The man motioned to the rows of barefooted survivors on the right side of the chamber. "These people saved themselves," he said. "They believed. And it's the same message I bring to you here and now—a message of faith.

"I couldn't warn them all," he said. "I am but man, a man of God, and He is God. Yea, the God of man. All those people, all those souls, all those dead—I'd give them all again tomorrow to see His mighty hand so raw, so wrathful, so beautiful. Yea, to hear His deep-throated voice, to hear it so clear and near—I'd give them all again, I swear it!"

The woman, David's mom, shuffled uncomfortably by his

side. He turned to her, his voice suddenly gentle: "Tell them. Answer your father's question. How did you live when so many died? Let them hear it. Let them be the judge."

"You saved us," she said. "Four hours before the first rumble of Mount Mystery, I saw him. I was on my way to work, to the forty-second floor of Magma Tower. I saw him, dressed as he is now, standing on a chair outside the entrance." She chuckled, as if thinking, *of all places.*

"He held a sign: *The End is Near.* A small crowd gathered around him. He called out to people as they passed. Somehow, he knew every name. He called out to me. 'Violet,' he said, 'let me save you.'" She paused and looked up at him, as if he were a silver-haired angel. "He looked so familiar. I had to stop. I listened."

Veronica glanced worriedly at her father. She wondered if the old jeweler was right. *An evil is coming—he's coming in white,* she mouthed the words. Her father shook his head. He did not believe in some kooks and not in others. He did not believe in kooks at all.

The woman continued: "He said anyone who follows him will survive, and everyone else will be dead by evening. I don't know why . . . but I would have followed him anywhere . . . I was ready to believe in anything . . . I had faith."

Her eyes glazed, and she continued as if entranced: "We left the building and walked through the city streets. Hundreds followed. We hiked to the top of Overlook Hill. With the entire city beneath us, we watched Mount Mystery convulse. We watched the top blow off. We watched the mountain collapse.

We watched the wave come. We watched it rise to our ankles, and we watched it recede."

She handed the microphone to the man in white. He thanked her kindly, then turned to the survivors on the right side of the chamber. "You are so brave, so very brave," he said. "You owe your lives to faith. You owe your lives to God. And you owe your lives to me."

Then, he turned to the gathered townspeople, his voice slow and solemn:

I know this news is difficult. I know these times are tough. But New Lava City was just the beginning . . .

We are returning to a simpler time, to a simpler place. The earth must be recycled. Balance must be restored.

I had a dream of a new earth—a new humanity, free of wickedness and greed. I have been sent here to share this truth—to invite you to a new world—and to warn you of what will become of this one if you deny me.

Here in front of you are hundreds of people, beautiful people, saved by faith. Under the waters of Fire Bay there are millions of people, unfortunate people, damned by disbelief.

I tell you this: On the third day of darkness, an explosion will arise from the nearest volcano, an explosion that will consume this town and everyone in it. It will be worse for you than New Lava City, and I can tell you those people did not drown with dignity.

These are the last few days of your lives . . .

"Liar!" shrieked a woman.

"Madman!" called another.

The mayor held up his hands. "Shh! Let him speak! Quiet!" he shouted.

The man in white smiled. "I know. I know," he said, his voice silky smooth. "But I didn't come to fool you. It is my burden to know the way. And I must share it with you, as difficult as it is. But know this: There *is* a way."

"Tell us the way!" an old woman shouted. "Tell us the way!" cried another and another.

Captain John looked around at the rapt and worried faces of his friends and neighbors. The man in white reveled in their fear, placidly twisting his long silver tresses around his fingers.

"The way is as hard as it is clear, and you must choose it for yourself," he said. "I cannot force the way upon you any more than a water droplet can force the rain cloud to thunder. I am but a mouthpiece, the prophet of truth. You have *one last chance* to save your lives, to save this town, to put an end to the darkness, and to bring to the earth a new light. You have *one last chance*."

The crowd swallowed his words like candy. "Tell us the way! Tell us the way!" it throbbed.

"The way is simple," the man in white continued. "When you walk out of this church, you walk into the first day of darkness. On the dark morning of the third day, you must bring to the volcano your most precious treasures, your firstborn daughters, every firstborn girl under the age of eighteen, every single one of them.

"Each of them must pack a suitcase, a single bag of things they'll need in the hereafter—their favorite books and clothes, pictures, and stuffed animals. Then, you must cast your daughters and their things into the fiery lava of the nearest volcano. Only then will the volcano be calmed. Only then will the sun rise again."

The crowd gasped in horror.

The Captain rushed the podium, grabbing for the microphone. The man in white offered it to him willingly, even cheerfully. He touched the Captain's forearm and whispered through a grin, "Maddy won't suffer long."

The Captain swung at him wildly. Two survivors leapt up to protect their savior, but the man in white raised his muscled arms. "No, no," he said calmly into the microphone. "We do not meet violence with violence. We come in peace. Let this man speak."

"*Devilry!*" the Captain raged from the podium. "This man is no prophet. He demands you turn your back on your family! On your neighbors! There's always a crackpot predicting the end. So he was right about New Lava City—so what! That doesn't make him a *prophet*! But what he's asking for, there can be no mistaking, what he's asking for makes him a *madman!*"

At that, the man in white nodded his silver head. Four large men in tattered clothes shoved the Captain back into his seat. "You mustn't interrupt the prophet again," one whispered, matter-of-factly.

Officer Steve now realized what he faced. Hundreds of people, goons even, sat at the ready, willing to do this man's bidding. This was no town meeting; it was an invasion. And now was not the time to fight, not with his firstborn daughter by his side.

The man in white retook the podium. A hurricane swelled behind the shores of his eyes, yet he spoke just above a whisper:

We are reasonable people, all. Nothing will be done here that you do not *choose* to do yourself. The truth can be hard—but it's still the truth. Following the way can be hard—but it's still the way. I can show it to you, but it is you who must follow.

I call a special election to be held tomorrow evening. It must be fair. Every man, woman, and child each must have one vote. If you vote to ignore my warning, then my followers and I will leave you to the darkness and to your fate . . . and we will mourn for you, as we mourn for our friends beneath Fire Bay.

But if you vote to save this town, I promise you this: I will make Crater Lake great again! But if just one selfish girl manages to escape the sacrifice, know this: It will all be for nothing. The sacrifice will be rejected, and you all will die. For this town to live, every firstborn daughter under the age of eighteen must die. It is the way.

On the left side of the chamber, every man, woman, and child rose to their feet, roaring in disapproval.

"I know, I know," he said. "But look around. The faith I asked of these people, these living people, the only survivors of New Lava City, I rewarded the same day. Trust in me, and you will live. Trust in me, and the darkness will end. Trust in me, and the volcanoes will sleep."

The plump mayor considered retaking the microphone, demanding by what right such a special election be called, by what right such a thing could be decided by a vote at all. But he remained silent, realizing what he must do. He would vote—the same way he always did—*with the majority*.

The townspeople streamed to the exit, united. Many even demanded Officer Steve jail the man in white. *These were the town's own daughters after all.*

But some minds changed as the church doors opened. What should have been a summer afternoon looked instead like the pitch-black night. At some point, after the Captain walked in but before the man in white finished, the thickening ash quilt smothered even the faintest trace of daylight.

The church bell tolled in its tower, ringing four times to mark the hour. A bitter wind howled across the lake. Red flakes swirled in the streets. Six inches of snow-ash mix blanketed the sidewalks.

"My family deserves a choice," Veronica heard someone say. "Maybe he's right," said another. "I always knew it would be Kaboom," said an old man. Most people said nothing. New Lava City was an unfathomable loss. Could it all be happening again right here? How did that man save all those people? How did he know?

Outside the church, Makenna had only questions. "Dad, is there really going to be an election? What if we lose?"

Officer Steve sized up his town. "I don't know, sweetheart," he said. "In my line of work, I've seen just about everything—bad and good—and mostly bad. But don't you worry. We're going to get you out of here. We're going to get you *all* out of here."

Veronica saw her chance. "Daaaddddyyyy . . ." she drawled. "Can Maddy and Makenna sleep over? You know, so they don't have to stay in town?"

The Captain cleared his throat. "Hmm . . ." he considered, "you know . . . that might be for the best. I've known these people my whole life, and they're some of the best people in the world. But the fear I saw today, I've never seen before. What if they start rounding up the girls?"

"No one's rounding up any girls," Veronica's dad said. "This is a good town, full of good people. When everyone wakes up tomorrow, when the newspapers write what that crazy man said, I promise you this madness will end."

"Maybe so," Officer Steve said. "*But would you bet your daughter on it?*" He turned to Maddy and Makenna. "You girls stay with Veronica tonight, and the Captain and I will join you in the morning."

"A sleepover it is then," Veronica's dad said. The lava car pulled up alongside them. Steve and the Captain said their goodbyes, and the three girls piled into the backseat.

On the short drive home, Maddy and Makenna exchanged nervous whispers, but not Veronica. Her mind was not on the church, not on the town, and not even on the sacrifice. With the girls sleeping over, she had her crew. She had the map, and she wanted the diamonds. Tomorrow, she decided, she would find them.

Darkness Day Two

CHAPTER 26

The morning broke in darkness. Veronica stirred in her bed, the tap-tap-tap of sleet unceasing on her window. She heard Maddy and Makenna snoring, snug in their sleeping bags, and checked her alarm clock on the bedside table. It was 8:00 a.m.

"Maddy, Makenna, wake up!" she yelled, tripping over them on the way to the window. "Oh no!"

"What is it?" Makenna grumbled. "Go back to sleep. It's the middle of the night."

"No, it's not," Veronica said. "It's eight in the morning. The man in white—he was right! It's the second day of darkness. Look!"

Maddy yawned. "Go back to sleep," she said. "Your clock is wrong."

"My clock is *not* wrong," she said, grabbing for the iPad. "Look for yourself."

Maddy grimaced at the bright screen. "Ugh," she groaned. "This. Is. Bad." She unzipped her sleeping bag and joined Veronica at the window. There wasn't even a glimmer of daylight.

Veronica opened the window. An eerie silence greeted her. Drifts of ash reached to the bottom of her second-floor perch. She beamed a flashlight into the darkness. Silver towers glittered in the light. "I think those are trees," she marveled.

"Hold onto my arm," Veronica said, and she stepped through the second-floor window into the ashscape. She sank instantly to her thigh, then to her waist, and then to her chest. "Help!" she cried. "HELP!"

Her mother heard her cry. She bounded up the stairs, barging through the bedroom door. "Get back in here!" she yelled, rushing to the window. Together with Maddy and Makenna, they reached for different parts of Veronica's body—an arm here, a shoulder, a head—until at last they heaved her back into the house, safe and sound.

"Have you lost your mind?" Veronica's mom screamed. "You could have suffocated! You could have died! It's ten feet deep. What were you thinking?"

"I-I-I dunno," Veronica said. "I didn't think . . . I . . ."

"Yeah, you didn't think at all, did you?" her mother said. "Now come downstairs. Your dads have been out plowing in Steve's pickup. They'll be back any minute. And breakfast is ready!" She stormed out of the room, making certain to leave the door wide open behind her.

"Geesh," Veronica said. "This is going to be even harder

than I thought." She grabbed for the iPad. "Maddy, I need to show you something." She held the screen so Maddy could see and tapped on a photo of Captain John's shirtless back. "Look at this!" she said.

"*Eww!*" Maddy yelled. "Is that my dad? *Gross!* Give me that!" And she yanked the device from Veronica's hands.

Veronica tackled her. "No! Don't delete it!" she pleaded, and they rolled on the ground, wrestling. "It's a treasure map. It's *the* treasure map!"

Maddy loosened her grip, and Veronica ripped the iPad from her. "I'll show you!" she said. "I'll prove it!" But instead of showing the photo again, Veronica opened the volcano monitoring app. "There! Look familiar?"

Maddy glanced at the map of nearby tubes. "No!" she said. A jumbled mess of red, orange, yellow, and blue tubes zigzagged in every direction. "I swear, Veronica, some days you're just too treasure-crazed. That doesn't look a thing like my daddy's tattoo."

Veronica glanced down at the screen. "Whoops," she said. "What about now?" She tapped a button to filter out all the hot active tubes, leaving only the cool blue, empty ones.

"Hmm," Maddy considered. "Now show the tattoo." Veronica zoomed in on the left corner of the tattoo. "Okay, now show the lava tubes."

The zigzagging lines of the cold lava tubes matched exactly, line by line, angle by angle, the crisscrossing pattern on the left side of the Captain's tattoo.

Triumphant, Veronica handed the device back to Maddy.

Maddy switched back and forth, over and over, between the tubes and the zoomed-in tattoo. "It's a match," she admitted, "a perfect match. Big deal! So he has some lava tubes on his back—so what!"

"Don't you see? What if they're more than lava tubes? What if they're tunnels? You see these two triangles?" she said, tapping the screen's left and right corners. "We know the left triangle must be under this volcano. It's too good a match to be anywhere else. And this other triangle, I bet you anything—it's under Diamond Island."

Maddy snickered.

"Laugh all you like," Veronica said. "But what else could it be? Why else would a tattoo be passed on for so long? You heard the story. The day before he died the Dreamer tattooed this mark on the Captain's son. Only he didn't count on one thing: that no one would ever figure it out!"

"Yeah, no one until you, right Veronica?" Maddy said. "I'm pretty sure my dad would know if he had a treasure map tattooed on his back all this time."

"How would he know?" Veronica asked. "All he knows is that the map connects him to Captain John the First. He doesn't know how. He doesn't know why."

Maddy shrugged. "Well . . ." she said, "on the bright side, if there *are* diamonds down there, maybe we can pay the man in white to go away."

Veronica nodded, although she somehow doubted it.

"Girls! Downstairs! N-O-W, NOW!" her mother thundered. "Your fathers are here. Don't make me come up there!"

The girls didn't dare ignore a spelling mother. They ran downstairs. Officer Steve had just plopped a stack of the *Crater Lake Gazette* onto the kitchen table. The headline screamed—in the loudest font newspapers use, the one normally reserved for declarations of war:

SPECIAL ELECTION TONIGHT!
Police Force Replaced!

The Town Council held an emergency meeting last night at 11:00 p.m. Following heated debate, the Council voted five to four to hold a special election to consider One Last Chance, a proposal introduced by the survivors of New Lava City. The four council members who voted against the proposal, as well as the entire Crater Lake police force, resigned after the vote.

The election will take place today between the hours of noon and 6:00 p.m. Every man, woman, and child in the Crater Lake tax district is encouraged to vote.

A flash poll of citizens reveals 65 percent opposed to the measure, while 20 percent support it and 15 percent are undecided.

"These cowards meet and scheme in the dark of night," said outgoing Council member Seth Harris. "They should be arrested! It's a travesty! Who can vote to murder children?"

Mayor Besboff disagreed: "True courage isn't always easy—or pleasant. Sometimes you must sacrifice the few to save the many. We can't let what happened to New Lava City happen here. All citizens deserve the right to vote. This is a democracy after all."

The Council also passed a resolution blocking every road out of town and authorizing the mayor to prepare a list of every firstborn daughter under the age of eighteen. "This is for our own protection," said Besboff.

In related news, as of last night, the three town grocery stores have sold out of milk, bottled water, and canned goods. Also, looters smashed the windows of the Village Bakery, stealing every loaf of bread.

"I campaigned as the law-and-order candidate, and lawbreaking will not be tolerated," Besboff said. "Given the resignations of the police force and to put an end to this crime spree, I've accepted the kind offer from the survivors of New Lava City to restore law and order. You will see them dressed all in white and stationed on every corner in town. We will get through this as we do everything else—together."

Maddy looked on the bright side: "Sixty-five percent! It's in the bag. We're going to win."

Veronica shook her head. "That poll was taken last night," she said, "before people woke up to ten feet of ash and another day of darkness."

"Veronica's right," Steve said. "And who's to say the vote will even be fair? That's why we've been out plowing—keeping the roads clear, so we can escape. But the ash isn't the problem. The goons are. They're everywhere. They're blocking every road. We have to fight!"

Veronica's dad snorted. "Fight?!" he said. "With what army? It's not the time to fight . . . it's the time to run."

The Captain nodded. "We'll run if we can and fight if we must," he said. "We know the terrain better than they do. But just in case, Steve, why don't you pay a visit to town? Check in with the other *Minne* captains. If it comes to a fight, we'll need an army."

"It won't come to that," Veronica's mom said. "We're going to win this election, fair and square. I'll stay here and dial for votes, starting with every name in the school directory."

"What can I do?" Veronica asked, knowing the answer.

"Right now?" the Captain said. "Nothing. It's too dangerous. Those goons could be anywhere. I need you girls to hang out here, stay safe, and don't, under any circumstance, open the door for anyone, and especially, do NOT, no matter what, go outside."

Veronica nodded her head and smiled.

The Tube

CHAPTER 27

After breakfast, the adults went their separate ways. Veronica's dad and the Captain headed out in the plow to search for unguarded escape routes, while Steve returned to town to assemble an army. Veronica's mom stayed home, dialing for votes.

Veronica, meanwhile, slinked up the stairs with her friends. "We'll just be in my room, Mom, if you need us," she called. Her mother didn't notice; she was midconversation, convincing yet another citizen to go vote and save her daughter's life.

Upstairs, the girls rummaged through a closet in the hall. Veronica pulled out three pairs of snowshoes, a rope, and a bucketful of winter things. "Now's our only chance," she whispered. "We have to find the tunnels. The treasure is waiting."

Makenna tiptoed back into the bedroom. "Are you sure this is a good idea?" she asked. "You heard the Captain. What if someone's spying on the house, just waiting for us to go out-side—alone? Waiting to throw us in the volcano?"

Veronica rolled her eyes. "It's dark out. They won't find us. Anyways, put on these earmuffs and wrap this scarf around your mouth to keep the ash out. Oh, and put these on too so you don't sink." She handed Maddy and Makenna each a pair of snowshoes.

Makenna backed away.

"Listen!" said Veronica, frowning. "Tonight we're going to lose that vote, and tomorrow, hundreds of people are going to come here for one reason—to throw us in that volcano. How do you want to spend your last day—sitting around waiting to be saved or searching for the biggest treasure the world has ever known?"

Makenna narrowed her eyes, thinking it over. "Fine," she said finally, "but *I'm* carrying the flashlight."

The girls readied themselves in earmuffs, scarves, and snowshoes. Flashlight in hand, Makenna climbed first out of Veronica's second-floor bedroom window into the ashy gloom of the dark morning. Veronica and Maddy followed, with Veronica holding the iPad and Maddy the rope. Together, they crossed the ash-filled lava moats at the edge of the yard and tramped up the volcano's steep side.

Veronica studied the iPad, switching back and forth be-tween the map of cold lava tubes and the Captain's tattoo. "The entrance *should* be just up here," she said, looking around. "But all I see is Big Ben doing his thing."

In front of her, a geyser erupted twenty feet into the air.

As geysers go, it was unremarkable, smallish even. But it was special enough to have a name. Her mother called it Big Ben because it erupted like clockwork—every fifteen minutes, give or take a minute. She would use it like a timer when watching the girls swim after school. "Okay, fine," she would say, "you can swim until Big Ben goes off, but then it's time to do your homework."

"Hmm . . ." Maddy considered. "That has to be it. Where better to hide a secret entrance than in plain sight? Who would be crazy enough to climb down a geyser?"

"You mean besides us?" Veronica said. And she watched the geyser water sputter to a stop.

Makenna peered over the edge of the gaping hole. She focused her flashlight on a small opening in the side of the geyser wall. "That's got to be twenty feet down," she said. "We'll never make it."

"We'll make it," Veronica said. "We've got rope! And fourteen minutes."

The three girls stashed their snowshoes in a tree, and Maddy wrapped the rope around its trunk. Makenna shined the flashlight into the geyser hole.

Veronica held the rope and stood at the geyser's edge. "Here goes nothing," she said. She disappeared into the hole. Inside, the gurgling rumbles of the inner earth grew louder and louder as she descended deeper and deeper. She scrambled down the wall, pushed off with her feet, and swung through the small opening. "Okay Maddy, now you!" she called up to the surface.

Maddy followed, making even better time than Veronica.

But Makenna hesitated. Her knees wobbled on the edge of the bottomless pit. "I can't do it," she said. "I'm afraid."

"I know you can do it," Veronica said, as the rumblings of the earth grew louder, "but you have to go now!"

Makenna put the flashlight in her mouth and gritted her teeth. She could taste its metal on her tongue. She clung to the rope with both hands, breathing heavily out her nose. She stepped into the geyser. *This isn't so hard*, she thought. *I can do this.*

Midway down the geyser wall, the rumblings turned to a roar. She felt a blast of hot air lift her skirt. She looked down. A white hot mist erupted toward her. She dove for the opening.

The lights went out. Makenna tumbled through the hole, knocking her friends down like bowling pins.

"Makenna, the flashlight!" Maddy cried. "Where is it?" But the flashlight was gone, rocketed to the surface by the sudden eruption.

"I have a light," Veronica said, "on the iPad." She tapped on her light and pointed it at the opening. The scalding geyser water rushed by so fast that not a single drop spilled into the tunnel. She looked for the rope in the surging waters but couldn't find it. She imagined it dancing in the fountain, still tied to the tree, and wondered at the chances it would come back down when the geyser stopped.

Maddy noticed the tunnel floor. "Veronica! The marks!" she exclaimed. "They're the same!" Two parallel marks about a foot apart extended as far as she could see, just as they did on Mount Mystery.

"We must be in this tunnel here," Veronica said, tapping on a zoomed-in photo of the Captain's back. "It should lead to a small room with five more tunnels. We should take the second one from the left. The triangle should be at the end of it."

They walked a few hundred feet down the narrow passage into a small chamber exactly as Veronica had predicted. They chose the second tunnel from the left, then walked another ten minutes. The cool tunnel air grew warmer with every step. Veronica assumed they were nearing the center of the volcano. She imagined lava gushing by, just on the other side of the stone walls. The air temperature exceeded a hundred degrees.

The tunnel emptied into a high-ceilinged chamber, about twice the size of Veronica's bedroom. Thousands of red-painted handprints reached out to them from behind the stone walls. Amidst the hands, a tower of four brightly painted blue horses greeted them, as if they had descended from the stars.

"I know what this is," Veronica said. "It's cave art. I saw it on a documentary. It could be thousands of years old."

Maddy gasped, not at the wall but at the ground. "Look!" she said. Hundreds of skulls, likely human, decorated the floor of the chamber like grotesque moldings. "Whoever this room is for, it's not for us. Let's go."

But Veronica continued into the room. She shined her light on yet another wall—this one lined with hundreds of drawings etched in stone, each one set in its own square panel. She ran her fingers over the deep etchings, then beamed her light from right to left and from bottom to top. "It's telling a story," she said.

The bottom-right panel depicted a triangular pyramid with a small circle on top, followed by panels of huts that resembled curved starships, set amongst the trees. The lower wall was covered with panels of dragons, monkeys, flowers, and vegetables. The middle panels told the story of childbirth and love, of friendship and death.

Two-thirds of the way up the wall there was a panel twice the size of the others: an etching of an enormous diamond, dazzling in the sun. Next came row after row of panels, all depicting diamonds—hunters with diamond arrowheads, beautiful women with diamond earrings, and sacred ceremonies of diamond-filled canoes.

"What happened to you?" Veronica whispered. She shined her light further up the wall, revealing still more panels—diamond roads, diamond huts, diamond temples, even whole cities made of diamonds. Her eyes moved steadily up the wall, until they stopped, dead, on one panel.

The light shook. Veronica's hands trembled. Maddy and Makenna looked up at the illuminated panel. Etched in stone, at the beginning of the highest row, the unmistakable face of the man in white glowered down upon them. He wore a diamond crown.

"It can't be him," Veronica gasped. "It can't be." She scanned the final row of panels, each one more horrifying than the last: motherless children, tidal waves, mass graves, then the final panel—children encircling a volcano, ready to be sacrificed.

The iPad slipped from her hands and shattered on the hard rock floor. Darkness descended like a curtain.

"I . . . I . . . let go . . . I . . ."

"It's okay," Maddy said, reassuring herself. "We can still do this, can't we? We can do it in the dark."

Even in the dark, the stone face of the man in white seared itself deeper into Veronica's soul. "It just can't be him," she repeated. "It just can't. I mean—how could it? I mean—it can't."

"Enough, Veronica!" Makenna said. "We're stuck in a tunnel under a volcano in the dark. Whoever that is, it doesn't matter. We have to get out of here."

"Yes," Maddy agreed, groping aimlessly for the others. "But how?"

The three girls found each other. They walked in single file with Veronica leading the way. Maddy and Makenna followed, each placing one hand on the shoulder of the girl in front, while feeling along the chamber wall with the other. Veronica used both hands, feeling into the blackness like an insect with her antenna, searching for the tunnel entrance.

Maddy tripped. A skull crunched under her foot. Stumbling forward, she reached out instinctively to break her fall. Her hand snagged Veronica's pearl necklace.

"My pearls!" Veronica cried. The necklace ripped from her neck. She heard her white pearls, the pearls her mother saved, the pearls her grandmother wore, clinking and rolling along the chamber floor. She fell to the ground, grasping blindly, but found none.

"I'm *soo* sorry, Veronica," Maddy sobbed. "We'll come back for them. I promise. We'll find them all. Please—where are you?"

The pearls continued to clink and roll, their clinking and rolling growing softer and softer and farther away.

Suddenly, a dim light lit the skulls lining the chamber floor. Veronica crawled to the broken one. It luminesced, glowing like no earthly light she had ever seen. She looked closer. It was one of her pearls, lodged in the eye socket and glowing in the dark.

Maddy and Makenna stood open-jawed in the white skull light. Veronica crawled to the edge of the chamber. She picked up another skull, revealing a hole, no larger than a penny. She put her eye to it.

"There's a room . . . below this one," she whispered. "The pearls—they fell through the skulls."

Maddy peered again at the wall of panels. A point of light spilled out of the top of the triangle in the very first panel— the one in the bottom right corner. It was lit from behind. She placed her finger in the hole and pulled gently. The panel swung open.

Hidden Chamber

CHAPTER 28

Just beyond the panel, a narrow stone staircase descended to a lower chamber. In the center was a six-foot tall triangular-based pyramid. Two of the sides were opal white, streaked with iridescent pearl. The third side glittered like a sheet of diamond glass.

The eerie light of Veronica's scattered pearls danced on the etched walls of the chamber. The girls approached the strange object, peering through its diamond glass into a hollow, empty core.

"Well that's the triangle all right . . ." Veronica said plainly. "But what is it?" She traced a finger along the object's smooth surface, looking for any button, any handle, any way in at all. Then, she noticed the tip. "Look . . . it's missing something."

"The circle!" Maddy said, remembering the panel in the upper chamber. "See here—the tip is curved, as if a small ball fits on top."

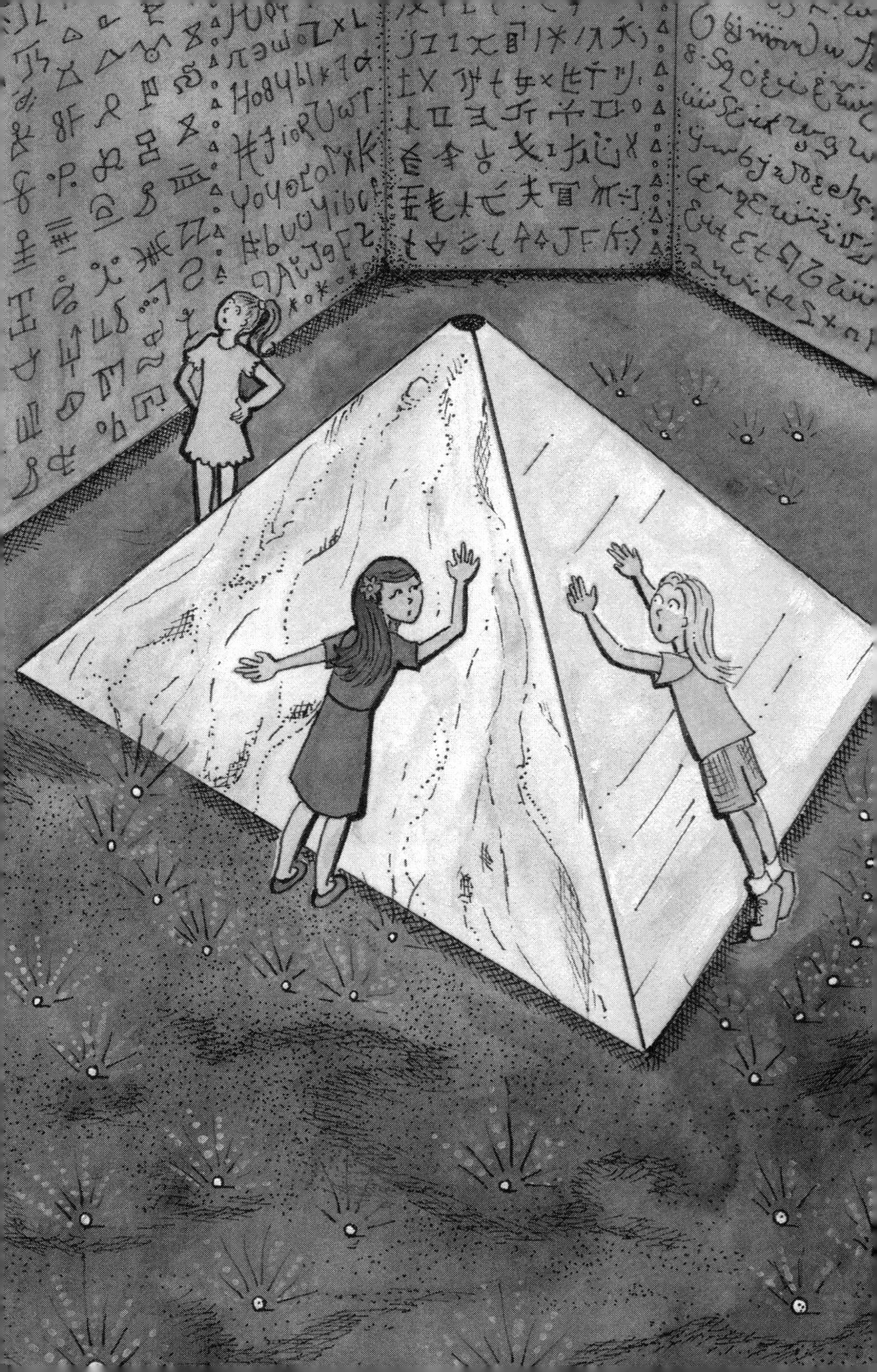

Makenna and Veronica looked for answers on the walls, amidst dozens of rectangular panels. Rows of markings filled each one. Some resembled ancient hieroglyphs, others familiar letters. The first row of each was the largest.

"That looks like Chinese," Makenna said, pointing to one set of markings. "And that, I think, is Arabic."

Veronica read the first line from a few of the panels. "*Ati-Ati, Tupato, Digtoonaadeen, Qaphela, Cuidado . . .*"

"*Cuidado?*" Makenna said, "I know that one; it's Spanish. It means *Beware!*"

"Beware of what?" asked Veronica.

"Probably that thing," Makenna said, and she backed away slowly from the strange object.

Maddy pressed her face to the diamond side and peered up to its tip. Her eyes traveled to the ceiling—to a panel above the pyramid. She read the unmistakably English words aloud, her voice echoing off the chamber walls:

BEWARE!
Here space and time bend
To no purpose or end.
Change what you wish
For good or for bad.
Beware fellow travelers
Gone murderously mad.
Beware reason, beware rhyme,
Beware this glitch in the drip of time.
Beware this doorway

Hear me now!
Beware asking why or how.
Run . . . run . . . run away
Forget this room,
Forget this day.
Time is just a dreamer's dream,
An entangled nightmare,
A screamer's scream.
Go . . . go . . . go away,
But if by chance you choose to stay . . .
If you dream of kings
And want to be . . .
If you dream of things
You must unsee . . .
If you must stop the pain,
Temporarily . . .
Then step in, step through,
See what this machine
Can do.

"I know what this is . . ." Veronica said. "It's the answer! It's how the diamonds were taken! It's why they were never found! It's how the man in white knew about the eruption! This triangle—this thing—it's a time machine!"

"Oh, please!" Makenna scoffed. "What makes you so sure—a bunch of spooky words? There's no such thing as a time machine."

"And yet, here's one right in front of you," Veronica said.

"Don't you see? It's how he smuggled out all those diamonds. The Diamond King took them someplace—or somewhere—sometime in the past or future. And now he's back. The man in white is the Diamond King."

"Don't be ridiculous," Makenna said. "If he really has all those diamonds, why come back at all? Why bother?"

Veronica glanced nervously over her shoulder. "I don't know," she said. "Maybe he knows we find this thing. Maybe he's here for us."

"Then let's destroy it!" Makenna said. "We'll tell our parents, we'll come back tonight, and we'll blow it up."

"And what good would that do?" Veronica asked. "Remember the other triangle on the Captain's back? What if it's another time machine? Come to think of it—if the man in white knew about this one, we'd already be dead. There'd be guards everywhere. We can't destroy it. This machine might just be our only hope."

"Our only hope of what?" Makenna asked.

"Of putting the future right again," Veronica said.

Maddy tried to imagine what a wrong future might look like, and realized, especially to the People of Wood, it might look very much like the present.

She stroked her chin with her hand, as if stroking a beard. "I wonder," she said, "what if the People of Wood came here in a time machine? And what if the Diamond King found it? He would have taken it for himself of course, but that wouldn't have been enough. He would have needed to protect the diamonds, not just then but for all time. As long as anyone, anywhere knew anything about the time machine, all his evil changes could be undone.

"So what did he do? He erased its memory from the earth. He killed Captain John the First, he killed the Dreamer, and he eradicated the People of Wood. Death kept his secret.

"But now that secret's out, and he's back. He has seen the future. He knows we become time travelers too. And he won't let that happen. Tomorrow's sacrifice is not about making the sun rise again; it's about murdering us."

"Then we have to stop him," Makenna said, "before he starts. We'll go back in time and make sure he never finds that other machine at all."

Veronica knocked against the object's glassy side, as if she were knocking on a door. "There's just one problem," she said. "We can't even get into the darn thing . . . but maybe there is something we can do. We can *let* him throw us in that volcano tomorrow. Maybe that is the only way."

"Are you mad?" Maddy sneered. "The only way? Listen to yourself! You sound like him: *The way is as simple as it is stupid, but it's still the way.* No! There's *always* another way if one of the ways is being thrown into a volcano."

"But don't you see?" Veronica said. "He sees the future before it happens. He moves through time, as if through rooms in a house. It's how he saved all those people. It's how he knows the sun will rise tomorrow. He's going to throw us in the volcano, and *voila*! The sun will rise again. The people will cheer, and his power will grow."

"Who cares about his power?" Maddy said. "All I care about is not being thrown into a volcano."

"But that's the easy part," Veronica said, smiling. "The trick is not dying."

"Anyhoo," Maddy said disgustedly, "tomorrow's tomorrow. And right now—we've got to go."

The girls crawled along the chamber floor, collecting all of the glowing pearls, sixty-one in all. Veronica put fifty-eight in her pocket, leaving three out to use as flashlights, one for each girl. They climbed the stone staircase to the upper chamber, retrieving the shattered iPad along the way.

They walked on through the narrow tunnels. At the geyser wall, they watched the water rage past the opening, then sputter to a stop. The wet rope fell back into the geyser hole, dangling within arm's reach of the opening. Maddy swung out over the hole. The three girls walked up the wall, one after the other, exiting the same way they entered.

Above ground, the pearls darkened in their hands. An icy wind bit at their faces. They strapped on their snowshoes and trudged through the ash, hurrying toward the light of Veronica's second-floor bedroom window.

Inside, Veronica's mom sat on the edge of the bed. Three pairs of eyes gleamed at her from out of the darkness. She leapt to her feet.

Surrounded

CHAPTER 29

Veronica's mother threw open the window. "How dare you!" she demanded. "I've been worried sick! I thought you were *taken*! Where were you?"

Soaked to the bone, Veronica climbed through her bedroom window. "Ma, it's okay. Were o—"

"Shut your mouth," her mother yelled, as the other girls slinked into the room. "Two hours ago I walked in here, and you were G-O-N-E, GONE. I searched the house. I called your fathers, and then, do you know what I found?"

She paused for effect, watching Veronica struggle with her snowshoes. "Three tracks of snowshoe prints right outside your window. I thought to myself, *No way would Veronica be so irresponsible, no way would she leave without telling me.* But I checked the closet, just to be sure, and guess what was missing?"

Veronica stammered, "Mom, I'm sorry, really. I didn't

think—" The front door slammed. Two heavy sets of footsteps hurried up the stairs.

"Yeah, you didn't think at all, did you?" her mother lectured. "How could you be so careless, Veronica? How? Here we are, trying to save you, trying to save us. Instead, I just spent the last two hours worrying, when I should have been making calls. I failed. I . . ." And she began to weep.

"I'm sorry Mom!" Veronica pleaded. "I should have—"

The bedroom door exploded open. Veronica's dad and the Captain came barging in. "Oh thank God!" they exclaimed in unison.

"No!" her mother raged. "Don't you dare hug them! They meant to leave. And there's no excuse! None!" she yelled. "You understand me!"

"You mean—you left on your own?" Veronica's dad asked, astonished.

"You left on your own!" yelled the Captain.

"No, well umm, yes, I, uh—it's just that we—listen!" Veronica stammered. "We don't have time to fight. I know how to stop the man in white. I have a plan!"

"Veronica, where were you?" her father demanded.

Veronica's mind raced. *Should I mention the map? The tubes? The time machine?* She knew no adult would ever believe it, so she decided to fib. "Umm, we just wanted to find a place to hide, you know, for tomorrow. We couldn't just sit around anymore, waiting to be saved."

"Oh, honey," her mother said, with tears streaming down her cheeks. "I know you're worried. I'm worried too. I've been so focused on the vote. But I was wrong. I should have asked for your help. You deserve the chance to save yourself. You deserve at least that."

"We're all waiting, Veronica," her father said sternly. "You have our attention. What's your plan?"

As if on cue, the phone in Veronica's room rang. Makenna recognized the number on the caller ID. She tapped the button on the speakerphone.

"Daddy!"

"Baby!" breathed Steve. "I got a message from Veronica's mom. She was hysterical. I thought maybe you were—"

"I'm okay, Dad," Makenna said. "We're all okay."

"Thank God!" he exhaled.

"Steve!" boomed the Captain. "What's town like? What's the mood?"

"The mood?" repeated Steve. "The mood is fear—fear of losing their shops, their food, their lives. They're afraid of everything it seems, *except* throwing a bunch of girls into a volcano."

"That's what I was afraid of," said the Captain. "How about the vote?"

"The vote's a sham," he said. "All anyone cares about is getting each and every girl into that volcano. They're worried the sacrifice won't work, that a few *selfish* girls will escape and doom them all. People are jamming every church in town. They're praying all right, but for what, God only knows."

"I can get more votes!" Veronica's mom said. "We still have time! The voting doesn't end until 6:00 p.m., right? We can do this. We just need—"

Steve cut her off. "You're not hearing me. It's already been decided. There's a list posted on the doors of City Hall, naming all the firstborn girls under the age of eighteen. Maddy, Makenna, Veronica—they're all on it. People have started going house to house. They're rounding up the girls. It's a mob scene. Someone asked me where Makenna was. All the wrong people are calling the shots. And they're armed. You were right. There's no sense in fighting, not anymore."

"But what about the other *Minne* captains?" the Captain asked. "Did you ask them? What about my brother?"

"Yeah, of course," Steve answered. "Ned is itching to fight. I'm heading to him now. But the others want no part in what is to come. They think the man in white is a nut job, sure, but they're not about to stick out their own necks—not with all these new *police* running around. We have to escape."

"Did you find any weapons?" asked the Captain.

"No, no weapons," said Steve. "They've emptied the armory. The man in white has a list of all the registered firearms. His goons are ransacking houses. I couldn't get within a hundred feet of the precinct. As far as I can tell, they control every weapon in town. Ned said he has two old spearguns he'd lend to the cause, but that's about it."

"Spearguns?" the Captain said. "An army's coming to the house tomorrow, and you're bringing us a couple of old spearguns?"

"That's right," he said. "That's all we've got. We're on our own."

Makenna looked ready to burst into tears, but not Veronica.

"Umm—Officer Steve?" she called into the speaker. "Hi—it's me, Veronica. Are you coming back soon?"

"Yes, of course, Veronica," he said. "And don't worry! There's no need to panic. We're going to get you out of there. We're going to get you *all* out of there."

"Yes, umm, it's not that," she said. "I just need something. Would you mind picking up the four black crates on the bottom deck of the *Minnehaha*?"

His tone changed instantly. "Whatever for?!" he demanded. "I'm on my way to Ned, and the *Minne*'s clear on the other side of town. This place is dangerous. Why should I?"

"Because I need them," she said, beyond explanation, "for tomorrow. Could you *please* just bring them?"

Officer Steve sighed. He knew it was the time for action, not debate. "Listen. I'll get 'em if I can, but there are checkpoints everywhere. I'll see you when I see you," he said, and he hung up the phone.

Her father looked at her, half angry and half confused. "I don't get it, Veronica," he said. "What's the plan?"

"It's simple," she said. "The man in white was right about New Lava City. He saved those people, and now they're his goons. What if he's right again? What if the sun rises tomorrow, and right on time, just after the sacrifice? Imagine how many more goons he'd have then. What if he knows the sun will rise tomorrow, but what if that's all he knows? What if he can't *make* the future happen?"

Her father's face brightened, as if a light bulb had gone off. "So *that's* why you need the crates . . ." he marveled.

"But, Veronica, that's *insane*. You'd die. Not to mention, no one can know the future. The man in white . . . he's just a crackpot."

"I don't think so," said Veronica. "And my plan will work—because it's the only one we've got."

"No," her father said. "That's no plan. It's crazy, and I won't allow it."

"What are you talking about?" Maddy interrupted. "I don't get it. What plan? Can someone just tell me—"

Boom, boom, boom. A heavy fist pounded on the front door, echoing up the staircase and through the open bedroom door. Veronica looked out the window. The headlights of two parked trucks beamed out of the darkness, as a half-dozen more rattled down the driveway. Men, dressed all in white, scurried this way and that.

Boom, boom, boom. "Don't open the door!" her mother cried. "They've come for the girls!"

Boom, boom, boom. "We know you're in there!" barked a voice into a megaphone. "No one may leave by order of the Prophet. You're to stay inside until the appointed time. The Prophet will come for you, when he's ready."

"Fan out, men!" yelled the voice. "Block every path away from the volcano. Cut off every escape. No one gets by. You hear me? No one!"

"We're trapped," Makenna said.

Veronica smiled. "Not exactly," she said. "You heard them. They're guarding the paths *away* from the volcano. They're not expecting us to run *toward* it."

Boom, boom, boom. "Enjoy your last night alive!" thundered the megaphone. "Tomorrow you die!"

The words reverberated off every wall in the house. The Captain had heard enough. He readied for an attack. The others did as he told them, closing every curtain and barricading every door. They turned over the refrigerator, the dining room table, bookshelves—anything heavy they could find, anything that could block doors and windows. But Veronica knew it would never be enough, that when those men decided to break in, they would, no matter if the doors were blocked or left wide open.

The sound of wild honking brought Veronica back to the window. It was Officer Steve, rumbling down the driveway in his pickup truck. Two men dressed in white stood steadfast at the center of the driveway. They raised their hands, signaling to stop.

Steve accelerated. He hit a bump and heard a man cry, then hit another bump and heard another cry. Steve pressed the pedal to the floor. "That's what you *git*!" he yelled. "That's what you *git*!"

Veronica raced downstairs and opened the garage door. Steve barreled toward it at top speed, as if he planned to drive through the kitchen and out the other side of the house.

He braked. Tires screeched and rubber burned. The truck slammed into the back of the garage, cracking the sheetrock wall, before finally lurching to a stop. Goons, dressed in white, raced toward the door, but Veronica shut it, just in time.

The megaphonic voice boomed into the darkness. "We'll

see you tomorrow—at 7:00 a.m.! Maddy, Makenna, Veronica! Sleep tight! Tomorrow you swim in lava!"

A head popped up in the backseat of Steve's truck—its hair mussed.

"Uncle Ned!" Maddy called.

He was fumbling with something long, thin, and wooden.

"Are those the spearguns?" she asked.

He nodded, passing her one out of the open truck window.

Steve, meanwhile, inspected his truck, checking for any dings or dents. He removed the tarp covering the truck bed, revealing four large black crates, the ones he had taken from the *Minnehaha*.

"Okay," he said, turning to Veronica, "I'm curious. Why did I just risk my life for this junk? Tell me—what's the plan?"

Sacred Ceremony

CHAPTER 30

Amidst the menace of another dark morning, the volcano behind Veronica's house buzzed with activity. At 7:00 a.m. sharp, dozens of large yellow buses carried the town's firstborn daughters to the volcano. Each bus had twenty-five rows. In each row sat a girl, a guard, her mother, and a guard. Each guard carried a club.

The man in white himself was the first one off of the first bus, flanked by one hundred men. His bus contained no girls, just club-carrying henchmen. Veronica peered at him from behind her front-door glass, steeling herself for what would come next. He strolled toward the house and rapped lightly on the door. "Come on out, girls! Today you save the world. You're the stars today!"

Veronica opened the no-longer barricaded door, suitcase in hand. Maddy and Makenna stood next to her, nervously shuffling their feet, their suitcases ready.

"Girls, it's so good of you and so brave of you to open the door . . . and so willingly," he said. "Now come with me." At that moment, a fifth-grade girl on the second bus shrieked at the sight of the volcano. She stamped hard on her guard's foot, hit him with her suitcase, and took off running. A stuffed brown bear, a pair of feety pajamas, and a framed photograph spilled out of her suitcase into the ash.

"Catch the girl," said the man in white calmly, "and punish her mother." Before her mother could react, the guard next to her clubbed her unconscious. He lifted her limp body up over his shoulder and carried her toward the volcano. The running girl shrieked again. Two guards caught up with her, snatched her up, and carried her away, kicking and screaming toward her fate.

The man in white addressed Veronica again. "See, not everyone shares your enthusiasm." He spoke harshly to the other girls emptying off the buses. "I have told you already. Any girl who runs will have her mother thrown in the volcano, too. Why do you test me?"

He looked into Veronica's eyes, his face as serene as a sunrise. He reached for her hand, and she gave it to him. She stepped out into the uncontainable night, willing her legs to move, one leg in front of the other, toward the volcano's peak.

Makenna and Maddy followed second and third in line. Two burly, bearded apes of men gripped their hands ferociously. The line stretched at least three hundred girls long, snaking up the dark mountain toward the mist-shrouded peak. Behind the girls came their families, sobbing and wailing, streaming behind them in mourning.

The flashlight-lit walk up the volcano took less than twenty minutes. The girls circled the gaping rim, still holding their guards' hands. The crater itself was a perfect circle, no more than a hundred feet across. But it dropped four thousand feet straight down into a thundering magma lake.

Maddy's heart throbbed like the dull crimson light beneath her. She recognized the unfortunate girl standing beside her. She knew her from school. They played together, occasionally, at recess. But try as she might, she could not remember her name.

The nameless girl spoke. "At least it will be quick," she said, terrified.

At least it will be quick. Maddy repeated the words in her head and looked down. *It doesn't look quick*, she thought. *In fact it looks like a long way to die.* She imagined counting to thirty while plummeting to her death. *I guess it's not much time really . . . to become a rock.*

She imagined herself as a blind stone, lying in a green field, reflecting the sun for thousands of years—without hope, waiting for nothing. She imagined some future little girl picking her up and holding her in her hands. *Would she even know what she held?*

"Too quick," the nameless girl answered her own question. Maddy reached for her hand and squeezed.

A drizzle started in the dreary darkness. From atop the volcano, Veronica saw more buses streaming in, carrying townspeople who came only for the show. They scampered excitedly up the mountain, cackling and laughing, flashlights bobbing in hand, snacking on granola bars and crunching on apples, chatting to each other about their dinner plans, about their rusted old cars, about whether the sun—really—would rise again.

The man in white cleared his throat. He held Veronica's hand and smiled at the crowd, his long, silver tresses aloft in the cool wind. "May I have your attention? May I have your attention, *please*?" The prattling masses quickly quieted. "Thank you," he continued. "Today is an occasion for great joy. Every firstborn girl in town is here, arrayed before you in a sacred hoop. Together, they offer their lives in sacrifice, so that *you* may live on. For their bravery, the sun will rise again."

The crowd clapped, and the man in white continued: "Did I not predict the darkness? Do I not stand before you now, the prophet of the living God? Who brings this terror to your doorstep? The Good Book tells us, 'The voice of God shakes the wilderness; He touches the mountains, and they smoke.' Who can deny God's will? With your vote, you believed, and by faith, you will be saved. Please . . . give *yourselves* a round of applause."

The crowd clapped again. Veronica studied the sea of clapping hands: the principal, the mayor, the softball coach. Then she saw David Hide Molten, the boy whose life she saved. His face was calm. His hands were clapping.

And she began to cry. The man in white also noticed the clapping boy. "There, there," he said, brushing away her tears. "Tears make nothing happen. That boy suffered. Babeltown suffered. And you will suffer."

His cold caress made her shiver. She glanced down at her watch. *It will all be over soon*, she thought.

The applause died down. The man in white continued:

"Now, before we perform the sacred ritual—before these brave souls descend the volcano and ascend to the clouds—we must say goodbye." He took a single red rose from his jacket, sniffed it deeply, and held it high.

"This rose, with its soft petals, its beautiful fragrance, its sharp thorns, is like these fragile children—impermanent—blazing through life—vital, colorful, alive! And like these darlings, its petals will wither and decay, feeding the soil so more flowers may grow. This is the cycle of being, the cycle of life. Today, these girls don't die. They live on in each of you, in your children and your children's children. Today, these girls save you. May you save *them* in your hearts forever."

He held the rose high and threw it down into the red, burning void. The townspeople clapped. A sister moaned. A grandfather wept. More lamentations rang out. As the rose fell, one father charged the peak, then a mother, then an uncle. In an instant, hundreds of people—all family and friends of the doomed girls—moved like a flock of birds, leaderless and one.

The man in white stood statuesque and ready. One hundred guards formed a wall. Wave after wave of fathers, brothers, sisters, uncles, aunts, grandfathers, and grandmothers came, only to be repelled, again and again. No amount of love, no amount of bravery, no amount of possessed fury could beat back the blows of the guards' indifferent clubs.

The man in white smiled. He looked out at the ring of girls, their suitcases covered with stickers of princesses and pop stars. He appreciated their agony, their utter hopelessness, their haunted eyes.

Around the rim in the cool mist of the dark morning, the girls faced the grim reality of their life's final moment. *If only more of the townspeople joined in, if only more people cared, if only* . . . Whether the sun would rise or not, they knew their end had come. Half wept. The other half prayed.

"Prepare the girls for burning," the man in white commanded. Maddy and Makenna felt their guards shove them to the edge of the volcano's gaping mouth. They felt their feet against the earth for the last time. Small pebbles tumbled into the black-red fire below. The man in white watched the girls dangle. "Assume the position," he said.

Veronica felt his hand on her shoulder. He pressed her gently toward the pit. Her head went dizzy, and her eyes clouded in white. Her nightmare had come true.

She slipped from his hand and leapt upon the nearest rock. "I'm not running! I'm not running!" she cried, her voice cracking. "Please!" She swallowed hard, choking. "Let—me—spea—"

The man in white nodded at two nearby guards. They raised their clubs. Veronica closed her eyes.

"Let her speak!" A thin, high voice rose from the crowd. It belonged to the old man, David's grandfather. His daughter, David's mother, shushed him, but he ignored her. "LET THE CHILD SPEAK!" he yelled, this time louder.

David's mom saw the man in white fix his icy stare upon her father. She knew she would not be alive were it not for the man in white. But she knew as well that her speechless child and her aging father would both be dead were it not for Veronica. She joined her voice to her father's. "Let her speak!"

The shouts turned into a chorus, as more and more towns-people joined in. The very people, who moments ago watched idly as the guards savaged their neighbors, now wanted to hear Veronica speak. "Let her speak!" the crowd throbbed. "Let her speak!"

The man in white checked his watch and shrugged. A single bead of sweat traced his oval face and dripped off his chiseled chin. He looked at Veronica. *Look how powerless and small*, he thought. "Go ahead," he sneered. "Speak up so they can hear you." He leaned in and whispered, so only she could hear. "Your sister will join you in the lava fire before the day is through." And he laughed.

The goons on either side of her lowered their clubs. Veronica turned to address the crowd. So many wanted her dead—but for what? She felt as if she were dreaming, paralyzed and powerless, yet perfectly aware. Her jaw locked shut, and her legs quivered.

"I guess she has nothing to say," the man in white taunted. "Let's continue then, shall we?"

An old, gravelly voice rumbled through the silence. The blind jeweler tapped his way toward the volcano's mouth. "I speak for the children," he said.

"Excuse me?" the man in white growled.

"No, I will not!" the blind man said. He approached the rock on which Veronica stood. She reached out for him, and he joined her. He stood before the gathered townspeople, and he uttered these words:

I had a dream the endless night
Burned and bled in volcanic light.
I had a dream your eyes so blind
Blackened behind your rotted mind.

You rot, you rot, and so you should,
Afraid of bad, afraid of good.
You rot, you rot, a slow decay,
Your life a debt you must repay.

Your cell I saw, your prison too,
I saw its bars were made by you.
Break free the chains, breathe deep the air,
Escape the bars, they are not there.

I had a dream, so real and true,
A different dream, as children do.
I had a dream of right and wrong,
Of yellow light and swallow song.
I had a dream the broken night,
Condemned to hell the man in white.

Beware the charms of this man's dreams!
Beware the curse of these girls' screams!
Unblind your eyes and see this man.
See his plot and see his plan.
He's here to kill and not to live.
He's here to take and not to give.

Nightmares end and so must this.
Lives must end but not like this.
Awake! Awake! Awake at last!
The present flows to future fast.
Love your daughters, love them well
Live the tale you'd have them tell.

A club fell upon the blind man's head. His dark glasses shattered upon his face. He dropped to one knee. His hollow eyes drifted up, toward a sky he could not see and could no longer remember. The club landed again. The blind jeweler toppled from the rock and bled into the ash.

The man in white wielded the bloody club. Blood spattered his pure white clothes. "Enough!" he said, yanking Veronica off the rock. "It *is* time!"

The townspeople buzzed. A chant of "SACRIFICE!" began. *The main event was near!*

The man in white grabbed Veronica by the shoulders. His thumbs dug into her clavicles. She cried out, and he mocked her for it. He lifted her over his head, bellowing at the top of his lungs: "LET THE BURNING BEGIN! Three . . . two . . . one . . . NOW!"

In an instant, Veronica, Maddy, Makenna, and every firstborn daughter in town flew through the air, pushed at the same moment, arms and legs splayed, plummeting into the fiery volcanic core.

A wail, like no wail heard before or since, shocked the heavens, fading like an echo as the girls fell. *One hundred feet, two hundred feet . . .*

Veronica looked up at the dark sky. She watched the stone-cold faces of her murderers rush away from her. She heard the townspeople, her own community, chanting the word "sacrifice," as she somersaulted, weightless in midair. The lava lake rushed up toward her. *Three hundred feet . . . four hundred feet . . .*

She understood the slippery ease of mankind's evil. And her breath burned her lungs.

Bang. Bang. Two shots rang out.

The man in white fell to one knee. He peered down deep into the fiery pit. He watched the plummeting girls stop, hang in midair, then bounce impossibly high. He rubbed his eyes. Yet there the girls still were—trampolining over a lava lake on a large, black net.

The rickety net stretched from one side of the volcano to the other, supported by four large hooks. Captain John, Uncle Ned, Veronica's dad, and Steve manned the hooks. Dressed in black from head to toe, they stood on opposite ledges four hundred feet straight down. Veronica's dad and the Captain laughed and waved, still clutching the spearguns they had used to shoot the net to the hooks on the other side.

"NOOO!" the man in white groaned. He pushed his nearest henchman into the volcano. "CUT THAT NET!"

The henchman fell, knife drawn, ready to sacrifice himself to kill the girls and complete the sacred act. As he fell, the yellow sun cracked the black clouds, sliding out of the ash and blazing across the midsummer sky. Veronica looked up and saw more than morning—she saw another chance, another life. She checked her watch: 7:40 a.m.

The guard bounced high into the air. Veronica recognized him as the man with the megaphone. The girls fell upon him, clobbering him with their suitcases, attacking with furious fists and feet. The guard let go his knife.

Around the rim, the guards squinted in the sunlight. They rubbed their eyes, as if awaking from a nightmare, tossing and turning but standing upright. They realized what they had done. The spell had been broken. Some fell to their knees, some stared at their hands, some cried to the heavens. All was confusion.

Unresisted, the girls' families seized control of the rim. Veronica's mother supplied the ropes. The sacrifice became a rescue. Guards joined with the townspeople. Together, they threw ropes over the sides and pulled one girl after another to safety.

Veronica, Maddy, and Makenna laughed and held hands, trampolining over a lava lake under a yellow morning sun. Atop the volcano, the man in white vanished into the vast and hazy stillness of dawn, as quickly as he had come, like a ghost in the mist.

Heart of the Volcano

CHAPTER 31

O ver the next few weeks, life returned to normal, bit by bit. Veronica's dad replaced the large fishing nets in the black crates of the *Minnehaha* with brand new ones. Giant convoys of dump trucks hauled ash from the town's streets, sidewalks, and lawns and dumped it in nearby volcanoes. Mayor Besboff and the remaining members of the Town Council were jailed, and the townspeople grappled with the stain of their vote.

Night and day, teams of people searched door to door, combing the countryside, hunting for the man who had made them monsters. They found not a trace, and Veronica knew they never would. The man in white's followers, the survivors of New Lava City, wept as the sun rose on that fateful day, ashamed of the people they had become, ashamed of their own hands for providing the final push.

Most of them returned to New Lava City and neighboring

towns, bent on redemption. They began the search for more survivors, pulling many from the rubble and saving countless lives. They vowed to rebuild the city from the ashes and restore it to its former glory. The people of Crater Lake supported their hurting neighbors in every way they could, providing food, water, and volunteers.

On the day after the failed sacrifice, the *Crater Lake Gazette* made small-town heroes of Veronica, Maddy, and Makenna, running a front-page photo of their smiling faces trampolining over a lava lake under a yellow morning sun.

People who voted to kill the girls would stop by Veronica's house, ring the doorbell, and beg for forgiveness. But she had none to give. She told them all the same thing: that they must forgive themselves first—that only kindness could heal them, the kindness they denied the town's own daughters, the kindness they denied her.

The newspaper reported as well on the plight of the savagely beaten jeweler. He spent seven full days in the hospital recovering from a cracked skull and concussion. Against doctor's orders, he returned straightaway to his shop. A crowd of well-wishers gathered to meet him, including a reporter from the *Crater Lake Gazette*. She asked him how he felt. "Still blind as a bat!" he told her. "Now git, unless you buyin' somethin'!"

Despite her newfound fame, Veronica was miserable. Worried the man in white would return, her parents refused to let her out of the house for any reason, including to go to town or to visit friends. Stuck at home with a smashed iPad and a broken pearl necklace, she spent her days at the window, stroking Lucky Bunny and watching the grey landscape turn green, one dump truck full of ash at a time.

Veronica wanted desperately to return to the tunnels, but not alone. With every parent in town keeping their daughters closer than ever, sleepovers were out of the question. But as the days turned to weeks without a trace of the man in white, even Veronica's parents realized they could not keep her shut inside forever.

One morning with summer fast slipping into fall, Veronica moped at the breakfast table. She propped her chin up with one hand, while swirling her spoon around a milkless bowl with the other.

The doorbell rang. Veronica decided it was more exciting than the table. She plodded to the door and answered it. There was David Hide Molten, the boy she saved, the boy who clapped. He wore a patch over his one eye. His grandfather stood behind him, two steps back.

She kept the screen door shut. "Why are you here?" she asked.

"Because I just wanted to say I'm—I'm—" He stopped himself. His grandfather nudged him. "You know?" the boy said, as if trying to change the subject, "I'm getting a glass eye tomorrow."

She clapped for him.

"About that . . ." he said. "About the clapping . . . that's why I'm here—because I wanted to say—that—I'm—you know—sorry." The word fell flat.

"Yes, you are," she said. And she closed the door.

"No, wait!" he said.

She opened the door a crack.

"Would you have saved me still?" he asked.

She looked him straight in his one good eye. She didn't want the answer to be *no*. But he could see plainly that it wasn't *yes*.

She shut the door the rest of the way and wept. She made her way back to the kitchen, plopping herself down, red-faced and miserable, in front of her dry cereal, just as her father strolled in to make his morning cappuccino.

"Who was that at the door?" he asked.

"No one," she said.

"It didn't sound like no one. I heard a car pull out."

"Well, it was no one."

"Okay then," he said. "Are you going to eat today?"

"What for?" she said. "I've done nothing now for three weeks, and I'll do nothing again today. What do I need energy for?"

"Look," he said. "There's fresh oranges. How about I make some juice?"

She shook her head. He saw her tear-streaked cheeks. He stood at the window, grating cinnamon into frothed milk and watching the sun beat down on the dew-sequined grass. He knew he had to put an end to it—that it was better to be hurt by the world than to be shut off from it.

"You know, Veronica," he began, "your mom's birthday is tomorrow. And I know you wanted to get her something. What do you say, we . . . stop by town after breakfast—and maybe—while we're at it, get those pearls of yours restrung too."

Veronica bolted from the room. Her father spun around, just in time to watch her empty chair crash to the ground. He heard her footsteps heavy on the stairs. He sipped his coffee, wishing there was more than one jewelry store in town.

Upstairs, Veronica ransacked her desk. She rifled through drawers, searching for her wallet, the green one, the one with all the money she had in the world: $43.47. It also held her broken necklace, all sixty-one loose pearls, and the volcanic heart that she had picked out of Mount Mystery's black sands.

Wallet in hand, Veronica tore out of her room, nearly colliding with her mother in the hall. "Sorry, Mom," she said. "But I have to go."

"I know you do," her mother said. "But *please*, be careful. The man in white is still out there, and he'll be after you."

She smiled and pecked her on the cheek. "Don't worry, Mom!" she said. "I'll be after him, too." And she bounded down the stairs.

Veronica's dad knew better than to dawdle. He had the lava car running and the garage door open by the time Veronica returned. She climbed into the passenger seat.

"Jewelry store, please!" she said.

Her father pulled out of the garage into a cloudless summer day. Veronica looked out the window with new eyes. Roadside wildflowers, flecked with ash, streaked by like rainbows; Crater Lake, as blue as the deep blue sky, teemed with candy-colored boats; and the townspeople, those sometimes murderous souls, ambled by contentedly on sidewalks, their faces bright with neighborly veneer. Everything was once again as it should be, or at least as it had been. Everything, that is, except for the sign on the jewelry-store door: NOT OPEN.

"But how can it be closed?" Veronica said, wanting to do anything—anything at all—but return home.

She tried the door, and it opened easily. Inside, the room looked just as before—if a bit messier. The same crayon drawings decorated the walls, hung this way and that, and the same musty smell lingered in the air. But the sideways mirror had been broken, radiating cracks from its center as if it had been punched.

She studied her shattered reflection in the mirror, then turned to the blind old man behind the counter, disheveled as ever, wearing new sunglasses and snoring loudly, his head resting on folded arms.

"Umm, excuse me, sir?" Veronica said, clearing her throat. "Are you open?"

The old man coughed. "What? *cough* Who? *cough* Yes. *cough* Come in. *cough* Of course I'm open."

"You know, the sign on the door says *Not Open*," Veronica's dad droned. "You won't get much business that way, you know?"

"And yet here you are," the old man observed. "What can I do you for?"

"I have two necklaces that need stringing," Veronica said. "You remember me, don't you?"

The old man pictured in his mind's eye an eager young girl with a small bag of pearls. "Can't say that I do," he replied. "But no matter. You remember me, I suppose. And that's good enough."

"Umm, I guess so?" she said, although she could not imagine how he could have forgotten her until she saw his head. A bump, a knot the size of a golf ball, protruded out of his forehead, capped by a thick scab of clotted blood.

Veronica approached the counter warily. "Uhh . . . here you go, sir," she said, spilling the pearls onto the countertop. "Can you string these?"

"Young lady, I can string anything." He felt for every one of her precious pearls. "Won't take but a second!" he said, his head bobbing this way and that. "And I have just the silk! Made by the finest caterpillars in China, very rare—very strong. Just got a shipment! The finest titanium clasps too, unbreakable. Won't take but a second."

But the old man took quite a bit longer than a second. He deliberately measured the silk to a length of five palms. Then, on his first try, threaded it through the eye of the thinnest, wispiest needle Veronica had ever seen.

He tied a miniature knot and pulled the threaded needle through a clamshell clasp. With a tiny eyedropper, he dotted a gob of glue inside the clasp before closing it. Next, he tied an overhand knot. "Now for the first pearl," he said.

Veronica's dad sighed, wishing he could be anywhere else on this perfect summer day. The old man poked the needle through the hole of the first pearl, without a hint of hurry. He tied a tiny knot and then proceeded, one-by-one, sixty-one times, each time pressing the knot against the next pearl with his long, yellow thumbnail.

Finally, he attached a second clamshell clasp to the other end of the necklace. He retrieved a pair of long-handled scissors from the loop on his belt and trimmed the excess silk. Next, he used a pair of pointed pliers to attach one of the clamshell clasps to a lobster clasp and the other to a small metal ring. He beckoned for Veronica.

Veronica turned her back to him. She tilted her head down and lifted her brown hair off her neck. The blind old man set the necklace on her neck and clasped it on the first try.

"Thank you so much, sir!" she beamed. "It's even better than before! And—if you don't mind—I have one more thing. It's a pendant for my mother. It's her birthday tomorrow."

"Is it now?" the old man said, as if he knew that it was, and he extended his open hand into the darkness.

She retrieved the heart from her wallet and pressed it into his palm.

He knew at once what he held. "The Heart of the Volcano!" he marveled. "Tell me . . . do you know its secret?" But before she could say that she did, he began: "The Heart is the most special pearl of all. It is activated by love. Whosoever wears the Heart becomes more loved and more in love. It is quite simply the greatest gift one person could give another."

Veronica's dad rolled his eyes. "That's funny," he said. "All this time I thought it was just a heart-shaped rock."

"All this time you've been wrong," the old man observed. "Please choose a silk." He placed a dusty wooden chest on the glass counter. Inside were silks of every color and texture, each neatly labeled: glowworm silk, spider silk, caterpillar silk. Veronica selected a black glowworm silk and pressed it into the old man's hand.

The old man felt along a shelf for the right mount, settling

finally on a thin piece of platinum. He bent and shaped the metal around the heart, positioning a tiny ring at the heart's center. He then slid the silk chain through the ring, completing the necklace.

"It's perfect!" Veronica said. "Just perfect. Thank you!" She reached for her wallet.

The old man heard the coins clang. "Your money is no good here," he said, waving his hands. "I know who you are, Veronica."

"But, you said . . ."

"Oh, please! You're all anyone talks about—the girl with the pearls, the survivor of Mount Mystery, the hero who stopped the man in white. Everyone knows who you are *now*. But what people don't know is who you are *next*."

She looked at him sideways.

Veronica's father spoke. "Please, sir, we would like to pay for these necklaces. You provided a service. How can you make a living if you ask for nothing in return?"

"What makes you think I ask for nothing in return?" the old man said. "What makes you think I make a living?"

Veronica broke the awkward silence. "Thank you again, sir," she said. She put her wallet down on the counter and held the pendant high with both hands. "Mom's going to flip! I just know it." She tugged at her father's hand. "Let's go home and wrap it."

"Yes," her father said, as they moved toward the exit. "Thank you, sir, and, umm, have a nice day."

The old man resumed his position. He rested his head on folded arms, as if another nap would do him well.

Veronica skipped out of the store, climbed into the car, and buckled her seatbelt. Her father backed the car out of its spot. Veronica patted her pockets. "My wallet!" she gasped. "I left it on the counter."

Her father braked suddenly. "Go ahead and get it," he said. "But don't dawdle. The car's running."

She bounded back into the jewelry store. Her green wallet sat on the counter where she left it, but the old man was nowhere to be found.

"Hello?" she called into the empty room. "I forgot my wallet . . . are you umm . . . here? . . . Hello?" She saw a shadow move under the closed bathroom door and assumed he would be out any second.

She approached the counter again, admiring the crooked, upside down, and backwards crayon drawings on the wall. *Why would a blind man have any decorations at all?* she wondered. One in particular caught her eye. She stepped around the counter for a closer look.

On tattered paper, a drawing showed two girls riding scooters, one red, one green, under a yellow circle sun. Veronica peeked at the words on the back of the paper: ELYSE, 4 YEARS.

How strange, she thought, not thinking her sister's name particularly common. She noticed another drawing, of two girls in dresses, a father wearing glasses, and a mother holding a baby. On the back, she read the words: ELYSE, 6 YEARS.

Behind that one, she saw another—a red construction-paper heart, its edges frayed by time, like something you'd find in the attic of an old man's house. She turned it over and read the back:

How Much I Love You!
You love me more than love,
But I love you more than that.
Happy Valentine's Day!
Veronica

She had written it herself just two years ago in the backseat of the lava car on the way to town. Ever since, it was how her family expressed their love. She repeated the line aloud: "You love me more than love . . ."

"But I love you more than that," the old man said, swinging the door open wide.

Her hands fumbled with the valentine. "H-h-how do you have this?" she stuttered.

"Really?" he asked. "Have you no idea?" He paused, straightening his crooked glasses over his empty eyes. "Veronica, I'm your dad. A little worse for wear, but your dad all the same."

She knew there was something familiar in his wrinkled face, something in the way his hands held the pearl handle of the cane. "That's *my* pearl, isn't it?" she said. "The one from Mount Mystery. The one sitting in my jewelry box right now."

"Yes, it *is* the same pearl," he said. "It's one of an entangled pair. In fact, this pearl and yours are so much the same that if you never picked yours up, then this pearl here would vanish. And if I destroy this one, well then yours would vanish, and so would I. They're the same. And *yes*, Veronica," he smiled. "I know about the time machine."

"But I don't understand. How do you have this? How did you get my pearl?"

"Not how—*when*," he said. "You gave it to me, or I should say, you *will* give it to me. You see, someday it will save my life. And I'm here to save yours."

Her head spun. "But I don't understand . . . if you're my . . . dad . . . then you knew all along: Mount Mystery, the man in white, New Lava City. You could have stopped it all. Why didn't you help?"

The old man pointed to the angry bump on his head. "I helped as much as you needed," he said, "and no more. The time will come when you understand. It's your job to shape the future now, not mine. I'm a time traveler, a paradox, a ghost. I live, if you can call this living, in constant fear, of saying the wrong word, of doing the wrong thing. You see, it's not my future to change, not anymore, not rightly anyhow."

"But why . . . why did you come back? Why are you here?"

The old man's voice softened. "Veronica . . ." he said, "how much do you think I remember of being ten? Of being a child?" He paused. "Nothing. I forgot. Children forget, and you will forget. You are becoming, Veronica, and I fear what you become. I have crossed the ruins of time to tell you this: The future does not turn out as you plan."

A tear spilled out of her eye. She smeared at it with her hand, sniffing audibly.

"My dear," the old man said, "let your tears flow. Tears are poetry—undiluted soul—emerging from us, like our fate. Tears make nothing happen. But what can happen without them?"

More tears streaked down her cheeks. He put his warm hand to her face. "You must never lose faith in the future, Veronica, even now. The future can save you, but only if you change it. Your life, I'm afraid, depends on it."

"What are you talking about?" she said. "Change it how?"

"You did just find a time machine, didn't you?" he said. "Or am I early?"

"Uhh . . . I guess," she said. "But I couldn't get in."

"Let's just say you figure it out," he said, smiling. "Trust me, you'll be a time traveler soon enough. But Veronica, when you get there, be careful. The future . . . *it doesn't like to be changed.* You see, the man in white . . . the Diamond King . . . he likes the future just the way it is. But he has a weakness. He is as blind to free will as you. He sees the past and the future, yes, but not the present. That is where you must beat him . . . in the moment."

"Enough!" she said. "Enough! I don't need clues. I need help. You came all this way. Just tell me what to do!"

He dug into his pocket and held out his hand, as if it contained the answer. He opened his palm, revealing something small and hard and wrapped in black velvet. He slipped the velvet away. A silver heart locket gleamed against his wrinkled skin.

"Never open this yourself," he said, "and no one can know where you got it. Do you understand?"

She shook her head silently *no*. She watched him feel into the darkness for her neck. He clasped the silver heart to the middle pearl of her necklace.

"This locket," he said, "will spring open at the appointed time, and only at the appointed time. But I'm warning you . . .

peek before that, even once . . . and any power this has to set the future right will vanish. You must not know even the time of the opening."

"But I don't understand. What happens?"

"Everything yet can happen," he said, raising his cane handle high. "With any luck, one day soon, me and this pearl here will disappear, another vanished time tinkerer gone . . . poof. You see, the future that brought me here—you can change."

Tired of waiting, her father, the younger one, the one in the car, burst through the door. He saw the old man raising his cane. He saw his daughter's watery eyes. "What's going on here?" he demanded. "Veronica, are you okay?"

"Yes, Dad, everything's fine," she managed, in her best nothing's-happening-here voice. "I was just, umm, getting my wallet, and we started talking about his pearl. It looks so much like ours. Don't you think?"

"Sure, I guess," her father said without looking. "But really, Veronica, we must go. It is time." He held the door open. As she passed, he glanced again at the jeweler. "Strange old bird, that one," he said, so only she could hear.

"The strangest," Veronica agreed, and she kissed the silver pendant on her pearls.

Get Veronica's Necklace!
FREE

1 Visit the author's website: **www.geoffreycook.com**

2 Ask your parents to follow the simple instructions

3 Get Veronica's necklace within 7–10 days*

While supplies last. We will give away at least 1000. Limit 1 per household. Free necklace with free shipping offer applies only to addresses within the United States.

GLOSSARY

Caldera   When a volcano erupts, the magma chamber empties, creating a large pocket called the caldera into which the ground above it collapses. Crater Lake, Oregon is a good example of caldera formation. The magma chamber beneath Mount Mazama emptied about 7,000 years ago in a tremendous eruption, causing what remained of the mountain to collapse downward into a huge depression, creating what is now known as Crater Lake National Park. Today, rain and snowfall have filled the caldera with the deepest lake in the United States (nearly 2000 feet deep!).

Cave Art   As long as humans have existed, they've been making art. Paintings have been found on the walls of caves dating back 40,000 years. Remarkably, whether in Indonesia or Europe, the earliest paintings look alike: figures of animals and outlines of human hands. In some caves, as in the Chauvet Cave in France, the paintings were improved over the course of thousands of years by successive generations of artists. Of all creatures, only humans look at a horse in the field and decide it must be painted. We humans began by painting our hands and drawing animals, and now we discern the equations that govern how gravity bends light. The human imagination truly is the most powerful force in the universe.

Clove   Cloves were once worth more than their weight in gold. It was the clove that sent Magellan around the world and Columbus across the Atlantic. Cloves are flower buds of the clove tree. The clove is currently used as a spice the world over. In some cultures, it is used as medicine to stop vomiting, to cure bad breath, and even to treat a toothache. For hundreds of years, the clove grew on only one remote island across a death-defying ocean. Its rarity ensured its value. Sailors would brave the oceans with one hope: to fill a small sack with cloves so they would never have to work again. Today, cloves have lost their mystique and their value, so much so that you'll probably find some in your mother's spice drawer. The clove tastes sweet, spicy, and intense. Bite into one (but just one!).

Doline   A doline is like a skylight in a cave. It forms when part of the cave ceiling collapses, often creating a hill at the site of the collapse inside the cave. One of the more amazing doline caves is Hang Son Doong in Vietnam. To get there, you must enter the cave and hike in total darkness for about a mile before reaching the doline. The sunlight streams in, permitting a jungle to grow. Life in a doline can seem pristine and otherworldly, uninhabited and untouched by humans. In Hang Son Doong, one area of the cave is called Look Out for Dinosaurs and another is called the Garden of Edam. There may be no closer place to Jules Verne's *Journey to the Center of the Earth* than Hang Son Doong.

Earthquake   An earthquake is the shaking of the earth, often caused by movement of the plates. The ground you are standing on is 1 of 17 moving tectonic plates. Volcanoes can often be found at the boundary of continental plates and oceanic plates, where the heavier oceanic plate dives under the lighter continental plate creating lots of friction and heat which melts rock, sends magma to the surface, and helps power volcanoes. Earthquakes can cause tsunamis and destabilize volcanoes, causing eruptions.

Entangled Albert Einstein referred to entanglement as "spooky action at a distance." It has been shown that measuring the state of one particle in one place instantaneously determines the state of a second particle in another place. There is no known force that can act instantly at a distance. Scientists instead describe the two particles in different places as one thing, as part of an entangled pair. Quantum entanglement inspires some very odd thoughts, like that space and time are not fundamental to reality, and that all of reality is potentially a hologram or even a computer simulation.

Extinct Volcano A volcano that can no longer erupt is considered extinct. This is different from a dormant volcano, which may not erupt for a long time, but still has the capacity to erupt and normally has erupted in human history. The volcano that today seems extinct might tomorrow come to life. A volcano near Rome, Italy called Colli Albani was thought to be extinct until it wasn't. It turns out its eruption cycle is just very long, longer than recorded human history. When it comes to volcanoes, extinct does not always mean extinct.

False Dawn   False dawn, or zodiacal light, is a faint white-blue glow caused by sunlight reflecting off cosmic dust from the interplanetary dust cloud. This dust cloud is part of the Solar System and is formed from asteroid collisions, comets, and other interstellar phenomena. The light can appear eerie or ghostly and is most common after sunset or before sunrise. Because it occurs in the hour before sunrise it has been confused for dawn, thus the term: *false dawn*.

Family Circle   Redwoods grow from seeds and also from sprouts that form at the base of a tree, especially when the tree is stressed by bad weather or by fire. The sprouts can cause a circle of trees to surround the original tree, creating a family circle. The parent tree may die and the child trees will live on. You can see these for yourself in the redwood forest at Muir Wood, less than an hour's drive from San Francisco.

Geyser   Geysers are found in volcanic regions where surface water encounters magma. The heat of the magma converts the water to steam. The steam rises through cracks in the Earth's crust and is ejected as steam and boiling water. Grand Geyser in Yellowstone National Park reaches heights of 200 feet and erupts regularly. Geysers are known to erupt following an earthquake. After the 1959 Hegben Lake earthquake near Yellowstone, all the park's geysers erupted including long-dormant ones. Despite what Veronica did, you would never want to climb down a geyser hole. In 2016, a man fell into a Yellowstone geyser and dissolved completely before anyone could get to him.

Howler Monkey The howl of the howler monkey can travel 3 miles through dense rainforest. They can be up to 3 feet tall with tails up to 15 feet long. They make deep, guttural howls and are considered the loudest land animal. Howlers spend most of their time in the treetops and eat leaves, nuts, and berries. Scientists believe these monkeys howl to mark their territory.

Lava Lava is the molten rock ejected from a volcano. Inside the volcano, this rock is called magma; outside it is called lava. The molten lava of an erupting volcano tends to be between 1200 and 2200 degrees Fahrenheit. Lava fountains can reach heights of one thousand feet or more. Lava destroys everything it touches, but because it is so slow, it is rarely the primary cause of death from an eruption. Most lives are lost to tsunami, mudslide, poisonous gas, and pyroclastic cloud. Most lava is red or orange, but molten sulfur burns blue, creating the effect of blue lava.

Lava Bomb Lava bombs are molten rock that explode out of the volcano and solidify as they fly through the air, landing sometimes thousands of feet from their source. They range in size from a few inches to more than twenty feet. They can cause injury and death.

Lava Necks Lava necks form when magma hardens inside a volcano. The hardening can cause an explosive build-up of pressure. Sometimes the hardened lava is exposed through erosion of the surrounding rock. Some of the most beautiful volcanic formations on Earth, like Pico Can Grande in Africa and Devil's Tower in Wyoming, are lava necks.

Lava Tubes The top of an active lava flow thickens from exposure to air, solidifying into a hard crust which insulates the rest of the flow from the much cooler air. The lava continues to flow beneath the crust carving out lava caves called tubes. Lava tubes tend to be between 3 feet and 50 feet beneath the surface and can be more than 50 miles long. The walls of a lava tube are often marked by flow lines, demonstrating the height of previous flows. Lava tubes often come in systems, with one system in Australia marked by more than 20 tubes. An easy-to-visit lava tube system is Lava Beds National Monument in California.

Lavacicles Lavacicles are a form of stalactite that take their name from their icicle-like shape. When the roof of a lava tube cools, boiling gas can force out liquids that drip from the ceiling and then harden, creating tubular structures of up to 6 feet in length.

Liquid Nitrogen While water is a liquid between 32 degrees and 212 degrees Fahrenheit, nitrogen is a liquid between -346 degrees and -320 degrees. Needless to say, it is cold. Liquid nitrogen boils on contact with anything warmer and envelopes that object in insulating gas. Liquid nitrogen is extremely dangerous to touch.

Magma Chamber The magma chamber is the source of a volcano's lava. It is a pool of liquid rock, formed by less-dense molten rock rising up through the cracks in denser solid rock. The chamber beneath Yellowstone National park contains more than 12,000 cubic miles of magma—that's enough to fill 1 billion 1-gallon containers 10 million times. Geologists map magma chambers using seismic waves created by earthquakes. Magma chambers can collapse or explode creating volcanic eruptions. Eventually the pressure caused by the pooling magma is too much for the surrounding rock and then BANG!

Mud Pot   A mud pot is a pool of boiling-hot bubbling mud. Surface water collects in depressions and is heated by steam rising out of the ground. Mud pots often smell of rotten eggs due to the presence of hydrogen sulfide gas. The gas and heat attract microorganisms which convert the gas to sulfuric acid, which breaks down the rock into thick, gooey mud. Mud pots come in many colors, including pink, depending on the minerals in the rock.

Pyroclastic Cloud/Flow   Some volcanic eruptions are explosions in which a mountain is blown up into pulverized bits. This fast-moving cloud of ash and gas is known as a pyroclastic flow. It can travel at over 450 mph and reach temperatures of more than 1000 degrees, destroying everything in its path. Pyroclastic clouds destroyed Pompeii in Italy in 79 AD. More recently, a pyroclastic cloud devastated the island of Martinique in 1902, killing nearly 30,000 people.

St. Elmo's Fire   St. Elmo's Fire is a blue or violet glow that can appear on the masts of ships or on any pointed rod, typically during a thunderstorm. It is caused by high voltage differentials ripping apart gas molecules and creating a plasma. St. Elmo's Fire got its name from the patron saint of sailors. Throughout history, it has been considered a good omen by some and a bad omen by others.

Stalactites/Stalagmites These structures are common in limestone caves. Water in the limestone dissolves the rock which drips out of the cave ceiling and on contact with the air leaves a trace of the original rock behind. When the drip is fast, it falls to the cave floor and deposits its tiny payload on the ground which builds up over time, creating a stalagmite. When the drip is slow, it deposits its trace of mineral on the ceiling, forming a stalactite. Stalactites can be 27 feet long and grow slowly (less than 0.1 inches per year). Stalagmites on the other hand can be 230 feet tall. An easy way to remember which is which is to know that stalactite has the letter *c* for *ceiling* while stalagmite has the letter *g* for *ground*.

Steam Ring Steam rings are rare, requiring the perfect conditions of a circular volcanic vent with individual puffs passed at just the right speed. As rare as they are, lucky observers of Mt. Etna in the year 2000 watched that volcano create hundreds of steam rings a day. Steam rings only last in the sky for a few minutes before dematerializing.

Supervolcano Supervolcanoes are so big they can cover the earth with ash and blot out the sun. They tend to have the largest magma chambers. The only supervolcano to erupt since mankind has kept records is Mount Tambora in Indonesia in the year 1815. It destroyed the entire region, killing over 70,000 people. The eruption plunged the continents of Europe and North America into a volcanic winter. In fact, 1816 became known as the "year without summer." As big as that eruption was it was nothing compared to Lake Toba 74,000 years ago. The Lake Toba volcano emitted 100 times more ash than Tambora, causing a volcanic winter that lasted 6-10 years and beginning a 1,000-year-long global cooling. Some scientists believe that the Lake Toba eruption nearly wiped out humanity.

Tsunami A tsunami is a massive wave that can be formed when the sea floor moves suddenly, causing the water above it to displace. While earthquakes and volcanic eruptions can be deadly, the tsunamis they trigger can amplify the death toll dramatically. In 2004, an earthquake caused a tsunami that killed more than 200,000 people. Tsunami waves can be more than 30 feet high. Before a tsunami strikes, the tide frequently goes out much farther than normal: a sure sign to run!

Tube Slime Tube slime refers to gooey deposits that coat the walls of lava tubes. This slime ranges in color from white to yellow to pink. Water droplets cling to this slime, making the cave walls sparkle under the glare of a headlamp. Tube slime contains many different types of bacteria, including strains that are used as medicines in antibiotics.

Volcano   The surface of the earth (the earth's crust) can be beautiful, but just beneath the surface is a fiery inferno. Compared to the size of the earth, the crust is just a thin layer that slides on top of a thick molten layer called the mantle. A volcano is a hole in the crust that allows hot lava to escape from a magma chamber. Volcanoes are the source of the earth's water, the source of the atmosphere, and the source of the primordial soup out of which life began. As deadly as volcanoes are, they are the source of all life. Without volcanoes, we could not exist.

ACKNOWLEDGMENTS

Of course, I must start by thanking the illustrator Gabrielle Shamsey. Her illustrations are works of art. I will forever be grateful for the life she breathed into Veronica and her world. Thank you Gabrielle!

I'd like to thank my daughter Madeline. Maddy wears a strand of pearls every day, even to bed, because her middle name is Pearl. She was born on Pearl Harbor Day. In her bedroom, amidst the Harry Potter hangings, you will find my poem on one wall and a photograph of a lava river pouring into the sea on another. She is kind to her sister and her friends. She is an artist and a lover of volcanoes. She wrote a poem to me and my wife for Valentine's day: "You love me more than love. But I love you more than that." I wrote this story to be read by her.

I'd like to thank my daughter Elyse. No one has more natural wonder. At age six, she will tell you that she plans to be a scientist and a rock star, and I believe her. No one asks deeper questions or more of them. She always has a song in her head, the song of the universe, vibrating on its varied strings, unheard except by her. Her hair is long-flowing and blonde. She has a love for curious monkeys, a passion for hot chocolate, and a taste for maple syrup that can distinguish Fancy from Grade A Medium. I hope a part of her stays six years old forever.

I'd like to thank my wife, Kerri. She imagined a little girl who lived on a volcano. She named her Veronica after her mother's middle name. She began telling Maddy bedtime stories in the first grade. Veronica's adventures were Maddy's adventures: a lost tooth, a win at softball, a skinned knee, a vacation to Florida. Maddy could not get enough Veronica. She would make me tell her a new story every day on the twenty-five-minute ride to school. Over time, the stories got more involved: fairies, mermaids, Diamond Island. Eventually I started to write some of them down.

I'd like to thank Captain John, Makenna, and Steve. They are our summertime neighbors on Lake George. A pillar of the community, Captain John does more than just captain the *Minne Ha Ha*, he fights fires and scuba dives. The patriarch, he is a keeper of stories and legends. Makenna, his granddaughter, is Maddy's friend. She is resourceful, full of awe, and always ready to adventure. Officer Steve, her father, built a ramp between the houses, creating one giant lakefront playground.

I'd like to thank the significant places that helped inspire the story, especially Lake George, where you can find the iconic *Minne Ha Ha* steaming past Diamond Island. Crater Lake, Oregon, was another inspiration and may just be the most beautiful place in the United States. We went in July and arrived in the middle of a snowstorm. There you will find cliffs green with lichen and water bluer than your imagination. I'd also like to thank Muir Wood for inspiring the Cloud Forest. If you find yourself in San Francisco, you must take the short drive to this sacred place. There you will find the tallest living creatures growing in family circles, with roots shallow and intertwined, each tree holding up the whole forest.

I must also thank the places I haven't been. The idea for Magma Pass came in part from El Camino de la Muerte ("The Road of Death") in Bolivia, connecting La Paz to Coroico. While I'm in no hurry to visit that one, I would like to visit the limestone pools of Pamukkale in Turkey, the inspiration for the limestone stairs. Another worthy journey is the Rio Celeste in Costa Rica, the inspiration for *Chowilawu*. The immense caves of Hang Son Doong in Vietnam inspired the setting of Captain John's grave.

I must thank the authors I read along the way, including Alfred Russel Wallace for *The Malay Archipelago*. His account helped me imagine the wildness of a volcanic region, still inhabited by natives. I must also thank the Blair brothers for *Ring of Fire*, both the book and the documentary. I owe them the term *People of Wood*, their reference to the tribe of cannibals who likely killed Michael Rockefeller in New Guinea. I also based my pirates on the *Dragon Prau* on the Bugis, the seafaring Southeast Asian tribe and the source of the term *boogeyman*.

I must also thank Simon Winchester for *Krakatoa* and for opening my eyes to the political, man-made fallout of volcanic eruptions, which in part inspired the man in white. In my research, I encountered the most stunning eyewitness accounts of volcanic mayhem in *The Last Days of St. Pierre* by Ernest Zebrowski, Jr. Those people did what Veronica did—they lived next to an active volcano as if it were commonplace. They heard it rumble nearly every day, and as a result, 30,000 of them died.

I'd also like to thank my editors Scott McCormick and Amy Betz for their valuable feedback and Shanna Compton for all her tremendous work in laying out the book and the covers. Lastly, I'd like to thank the early readers for their time and feedback, like Elena, Clara, Sophia, my mother, and my sister. I'd especially like to thank Elena for the idea of the glossary. Good idea, Elena!

I hope you enjoyed it, and thank you for reading!

ABOUT THE AUTHOR

Geoffrey Cook started telling *Veronica and the Volcano* stories to pass the time with his daughter Madeline on the twenty-five-minute drive to school every morning. She enjoyed his stories, and so he wrote them down. Geoffrey is a serial entrepreneur. He is the CEO and co-founder of The Meet Group (NASDAQ: MEET) and previously founded EssayEdge and ResumeEdge from a Harvard dorm. He lives in Princeton, NJ, with his wife, two daughters, and son. To contact him, visit www.geoffreycook.com.

ABOUT THE ILLUSTRATOR

Gabrielle McCaffrey Shamsey lives in Pennington, NJ with her husband and two sons. She studied figure drawing for three years in a classical atelier program, learning the fundamentals of art realism. She incorporates those skills into her illustrations, specifically regarding composition and character expressions. Gabrielle is greatly inspired by the artwork of Maurice Sendak and Ray Cruz.